MW01600646

A Killer Birthday

THE CHARLES BENTLEY MYSTERIES, Volume 7

Glen Ebisch

Published by As You Like It Press, 2022.

A KILLER BIRTHDAY

First edition. May 19, 2022.

Written by Glen Ebisch.

Table of Contents

Chapter One

Charles Bentley sat at the table and stared at the cake in front of him. There were seven candles burning on it, each representing a decade that he had lived. The number of candles had been by his request because a candle for each year would have been a bonfire rather than a birthday cake. He took in a deep breath and made a wish. Then he blew out all the candles with comparative ease. There was suitable applause from those around the table, louder from his two grandsons, Jack and Kevin. Kevin, who had just turned five, had asked how old he was since there were only seven candles on his cake. Charles had told him he was seventy, and the boy's eyes had grown wide, as if lasting for such a number of years was incomprehensible.

It was rather incomprehensible to Charles as well. As the day approached, he found himself trying more and more to distinguish each year of his life from the next, as if breaking his lifetime down into memorable segments would make it more comprehensible to him where all the time had gone. But all he had ended up with was a blur of homogeneous years, and all that stood out were a few occasions that had been of greater significance than the others. People often said that you had to seize the moment, but for Charles that had always seemed like trying to grab water in your fist. The best you could do to make time meaningful, he had now come to understand, was to set goals the achievement of which would bring happiness and strive every day to accomplish those goals. That took persistence and discipline, and these were two qualities that he knew he possessed in abundance.

In addition to the boys, seated around the table in the small room they had to themselves off the main dining room in Chasborne's restaurant were Joanna, his wife of just a year, who was also the chief of police in the town of Opalsville in the upper western corner of Massachusetts; his daughter, Amy; and her fiancé, Sanjay. There were a few others who also would have happily attended, particularly Yuri Abramovitch, the chair of the English Department at Opal College where Charles had taught for many years until his recent retirement. Yuri would have been delighted to embark on a lengthy encomium about Charles, but given Yuri's weak grasp of the American vernacular, that would probably have turned the evening into a roast.

Charles had wanted to keep the event small because he wasn't certain how he felt about getting older. He was moderately optimistic about the future, but he also found himself well aware of the diminishing number of years that were probably allotted to him. That didn't stop him from making plans, but most of his plans now had a shorter horizon line.

The feeling he had was somewhat similar to the way he had felt upon nearing the end of one of the articles or books that he had written in his field of American literature. As you closed in on the conclusion, you could take satisfaction in looking back on all that had been accomplished so far, but at the same time you felt a driving need to make certain that the conclusion would strongly reinforce the important points that you'd made so far in the text. He wanted to conclude his life with a dramatic coda that would demonstrate to others what it had all been about.

Joanna touched his hand to indicate that it was time to cut the cake before the boys dove into it with their hands. Charles ceremoniously cut the cake, making sure that the boys received portions that were probably far larger than they could ever eat. Amy gave him a slightly admonishing glance, but spoiling grandchildren was one of the small pleasures of old age. As everyone ate and said complimentary things about the cake, Charles sipped his coffee and enjoyed the present moment of being with his family. After having a second cup of coffee, Charles decided that he'd better visit the restroom, a slight diminishment of bladder control being one of the less pleasurable aspects of increasing years.

Charles excused himself and headed toward the front of the restaurant. The restrooms were down a short hall right inside the front door. He had just finished and turned away from the urinal when the door to the restroom opened. A man came inside, stumbling backward. At first, Charles thought he must have been talking to someone behind him, but then he realized that the man was alone. The man turned so that he and Charles were momentarily facing each other. Charles noticed that the man had a peculiar red decoration on his chest. He gave the man a nod and in response, the man reached out toward him.

6

"Help," the man said, and then with a twisting motion he fell to the floor, settling on his back.

Charles knelt down beside him, not certain what to do. The man's eyes were open, staring at the ceiling, and now Charles realized that the red decoration was blood. Taking a deep breath, he stood and made his way back to the room where they were having the celebration. Joanna looked up as he entered, and he motioned for her to come to him.

"What's the matter, Charles?" she asked, joining him by the door. "You look like you've seen a ghost."

"I think someone just died in the men's room."

Joanna gave him a quick look to be certain he was serious, and then she turned to the room where everyone was seated, looking at her expectantly.

"We'll be right back," she announced in a no-nonsense voice.

Charles and Joanna strolled casually across the restaurant dining room. Charles looked about him thinking how much disruption was soon going to be unleashed upon the owners, the staff, and the patrons. His birthday would certainly be a memorable day for them.

"Don't let anyone else in," Joanna ordered Charles, as she opened the door and entered the men's room

Fortunately, no one came along who needed the facilities, and in a few minutes, Joanna reappeared.

"Unfortunately, you're right. The man is dead. I've called for more officers. We'll have to question everyone here."

"How did he die? I saw some blood."

"I'll have to wait for the medical examiner, but it looks to me like a stab wound. Would you get Amy and the boys and Sanjay back home? I can question them on my own, and I'm pretty sure they didn't see anything since they were with us the entire evening. I'll wait here for the team to arrive."

Charles returned to the room and told the small group that Joanna had to leave for work-related reasons, and perhaps it would be best if they went home now. Their waitress returned to box up the cake, and Charles paid the bill. Clearly, Joanna had managed to limit the panic so far, but it would only be a matter of minutes before confusion would reign.

As Charles hustled them out the door into the main restaurant area, he could already hear sirens in the distance.

Jack pulled on his hand. "Hey, Grandpa," he said. "That was a killer birthday, wasn't it?"

Charles gave a rueful smile. "Indeed it was."

"What's wrong?" Amy asked, as they walked to the car.

She and Charles were several feet behind Sanjay, who had a boy holding each hand and tugging in opposite directions.

Charles lowered his voice. "A man entered the restroom when I was in there, and he apparently died on the floor."

"Why do these things always happen to you?" Amy asked accusingly.

"I don't know, but it's not my fault."

"I guess not," she admitted grudgingly. "Did he have a heart attack or stroke?"

Charles paused, wanting to delay this moment for as long as possible

"Joanna thinks he was stabbed."

Amy gave him a level look. "So here we go again."

"I'm afraid so."

Chapter Two

Charles went to bed at his usual time of eleven o'clock. He wasn't particularly sleepy, still being keyed up over seeing a man die, but Joanna was at work, and he couldn't think of anything better to do. Jeff, the owner at the Flight or Fight Gym where he trained, had told him that one of the most important things for good health was to have a regular sleep schedule. So it was very important to go to bed at the same time every night. Although he'd been something of a night owl in his earlier years, Charles had noticed that as he'd gotten older, he often felt his energy decline in the middle of the day. Therefore, he'd taken Jeff's advice to heart, and even though he sometimes woke up rather early in the morning, he had found that he generally felt better for going to bed at a reasonable time.

He'd heard Joanna come to bed somewhere around two, but he'd quickly turned over and gone back to sleep, relieved that she had returned home. Although he'd only been married a year, he found it comforting to share a bed with another person. Oddly, since the death of his first wife, Barbara, several years ago, he'd felt lonelier alone in bed at night than during the day. He wondered if even when asleep we were aware on some level of the person next to us and felt her absence.

The next morning, Charles had finished his breakfast of oatmeal and toast and was savoring his second cup of coffee when Joanna appeared dressed in uniform and ready for the day.

"Would you like some coffee?" he asked, reaching behind him for the pot.

"Yes, I think I'll be needing that," she replied, popping a piece of bread in the toaster.

"Would you like me to scramble a couple of eggs?" he asked.

She shook her head. "I have to show up on time, even though I worked late. The first day of a murder investigation is always the most important one, and I want to motivate the team."

"Isn't that the job of your chief of detectives?"

"He's away on vacation this week, so I'm taking over."

"I'm sure you'll hate that," Charles said, giving her a mischievous smile. It was a joke between them that one of the things Joanna liked least about her promotion to police chief is that she had become an administrator more than an active detective.

She smiled. "But this could be a tough case."

"What do you know so far?"

"The murdered man is Raymond Harris. He was a lawyer with Barlow, Harris, and Royce. We learned that much from looking through his wallet."

Charles gave a whistle of surprise. "Barlow, Harris, and Royce is the premier law firm in Opalsville. They handle all the legal work for Opal College."

"Yeah, I think they even have a lot of out-of-state clients. Folks from New York City who have summer homes up here use them for local real estate transactions. They've been around a long time and have deep roots in the community."

"So that will make it an important case."

"One of the senior partners turning up murdered is going to put a lot of pressure on the department. The mayor has already sent me one of his typical panicked text messages. Someone must call him in the middle of the night to let him know about this stuff."

"Someone should call him about all the potholes in the center of town. That's a problem he might be able to solve instead of spending his time harassing you."

"Spoken like a good husband," Joanna said, biting into her toast.

"Did anyone at the restaurant see anything?"

"Actually, we had a little luck there. The hostess at the restaurant was standing near the front door when Harris entered. He didn't come into the dining room but turned to head directly for the men's room. But she noticed him because he staggered slightly as he walked, and she was afraid that he might be drunk. She made a mental note to herself to have one of the waiters check in the men's room if he didn't come out in a few minutes."

"Was he all by himself?"

"As far as she could tell, he was alone. And the reservation was made in his name, so we have no way of knowing if he was meeting anyone."

"Chasborne's is a pretty expensive place to go to dine by yourself." Charles pointed out.

Joanna shrugged. "Harris was recently divorced. We found that out when we called one of his partners last night. He lived alone, so maybe eating out was a treat he gave to himself."

"I'm sure he could afford it. Did the attending doctor agree with you that he died from a stab wound?"

"Dr. Bell said he wouldn't know for sure what the cause of death was until the body had been opened up, but he was certain that a stab wound to the heart had been inflicted."

"I'm surprised that Harris was able to walk around after being stabbed in the heart. Wouldn't something like that put you down immediately?"

"I thought the same thing. Bell said that would certainly be true if you were stabbed in the right ventricle and the weapon was removed. Then the heart would almost immediately drown in blood. But if it hit the left ventricle, which is thicker and seals better, you might be able to walk around for a bit, although you wouldn't be running any marathons."

"So do you know where Harris was when he was attacked?"

"One of our keen-eyed forensics people spotted a few drops of blood on the sidewalk about twenty feet from the front door of the restaurant."

"Do you think it was a mugging? Some guy who figures that people who go to Chasborne's have lots of money on them, so he goes to rob a guy and things go south. My recollection from the one time I saw him is that Harris was a pretty big man."

"Six-one. Yeah, he might have put up a fight and gotten stabbed for his efforts." Joanna agreed.

"Of course, there's another possibility."

"What's that?"

"Well, when you really think about it, making a dinner reservation to meet with someone is a good way of getting them to a particular place at a particular time. As I recall, there are no windows from the restaurant looking out onto the front walk, so it would be a handy spot to kill someone. There are trees all around, and no view from the road."

Joanna paused to give the idea some thought.

"Maybe, but it would certainly be risky. What if some other diners arrived at the same time?"

"What time was Harris's reservation?"

11

"Eight o'clock."

"That's pretty late. It's right around sunset now that we're toward the end of August. Maybe the killer was betting that things would have slowed down by then. You rush out from your car to meet him as he's walking up to the restaurant. You call out hello, and he turns to greet you. You plunge the knife into his heart and then turn and walk away. It's over in a matter of seconds and no one is the wiser."

"It takes a pretty cool killer to pull off something like that."

"So your choice is between a nervous mugger or a cold-blooded killer. How do you find out which it is?" Charles asked.

"Police work. We find out as much about the victim as we can. I've got an appointment this morning with Attorney Jonathan Royce, the managing partner at Barlow, Harris, and Royce. I'm hoping he can tell me more about his colleague's life and hopefully his enemies."

"I know Royce. We were on a committee at the college together setting up the new sexual harassment policy. He seems to be a reasonable guy. We had lunch together a couple of times. He has a real interest in Hemingway."

Joanna gave him a speculative glance. "How would you like to come along with me for the interview?"

"Isn't it unusual to have a civilian along?"

"Yes, but with the chief detective away, it's either you or a junior officer in his twenties who will feel like he's suddenly eating at the adult table. I think you'll be of more use."

"I know that's why you keep me around. Because I come in useful."

Joanna smiled. "In so many ways."

Chapter Three

Charles sat in his study in the spacious right front room of his house and watched a steady string of people walking past heading toward the downtown. When he had moved from further out in the country into the center of Opalsville a year ago, he had wondered how he would feel about being so close to other people. There was an obvious value to being within walking distance of the essentials of life, but in his previous house, he could look out on woods and meadows extending as far as the eye could see and not spot another person for days at a time. Before he moved, he had wondered if he would miss the solitude. His conclusion, as of right now, was that he actually enjoyed watching others. He would see them plodding, strolling, running, and striding along with a variety of expressions on their faces, and take great satisfaction in imagining what they were thinking and what sort of lives they led.

It reminded him of a time when he had done graduate research in New York, and the elevated train into the city had taken him slowly past the second floors of rows of tenements, where he had been able to glance into the windows of kitchens, bedrooms, and living rooms, catching snapshots of lives in the act of being lived. For an instant, you felt yourself to be in those rooms and became a part of a very different life from your own. It was disorienting but at the same time fascinating.

Charles wondered if his curiosity about people had always been there but had been repressed by his more abstract interest in literature. Had it only been recently released since he'd started writing mystery fiction and switched from studying the general to the particular? Was it a variation of the old saying that for a man who has a hammer, every problem looks like a nail? Does a man who writes mysteries see every person as a potential story? He didn't think that was quite true in his case, but Charles would admit that his turn toward fiction had made everyone around him seem much more complex, a bustling bundle of conflicting motivations; much like a physicist describes the world of objects as being swirling clouds of atoms. This might truly be the way people and things really are, but to experience life that way challenges our sense of a stable world, where things are real and people are usually as they appear to be.

His first book had recently been published under the title of *Vengeance*. The title was the publisher's choice. His editor at Too Many Corpses Press had told him that readers preferred books with direct rather than subtle titles. Charles thought it could equally well have been called *Justice* because in a way the two shared a sort of equivalence. If the pain inflicted on the perpetrator didn't at least approximate the suffering caused by the crime, a sense of imbalance would come to permeate society. Because that imbalance was too often the case given the imperfections of human justice, people enjoyed mysteries because, at least in most of them, the world returned to being an orderly place at the end.

He knew he should settle down and create a marketing plan for his book. His editor had told him in so many words that marketing and advertising were up to him. They would edit and publish the book, but whether anyone beyond friends and family read it was dependent on his own efforts. Although it seemed wrong that someone who just wanted to write stories had to become an entrepreneur, that was apparently the way of the world in publishing today, so he was starting to carefully dip a toe into the alien ocean of online advertising. He was starting, as any traditionalist would, by reading as much as possible about the subject.

An hour later, he looked up from this reading relieved to see that he could start getting ready to meet Joanna at the offices of Barlow, Harris, and Royce. He dressed in a suit, which he rarely had done since his retirement, because he felt that lawyers would be more likely to see him as an equal if he were in formal attire. There was also the fact that Joanna would be resplendent in her uniform, and he didn't want to let down his side.

The offices of Barlow, Harris, and Royce turned out to be located in a large brick house—more of a mansion actually—just north of downtown Opalsville. The third-floor office occupied by Jonathan Royce had an expansive view northward toward the hills of Vermont, and Charles had found his attention wandering to their natural beauty ever since a secretary had escorted them into the office. Charles and Royce had exchanged a friendly handshake and a few words based on past experiences together at the college and proper condolences for Harris's passing had been expressed all around. Charles could tell that now Joanna was ready to get down to business.

"So you, Mr. Harris, and Mr. Barlow are the senior partners in the law firm?" she asked.

"Well, actually, Mr. Barlow is no longer with us."

She raised a quizzical eyebrow.

"He was the founding partner and forty years older than Harris and myself. He passed away almost ten years ago. As is a tradition with many law firms, we've kept the name of the founding partner on the wall so to speak."

"But you were next in seniority and that's why you became managing partner?"

He shook his head. "Actually, Harris began with the firm about five years before I did, and for some time he was the managing partner after Barlow turned the reins over to us. But a few years ago, he grew tired of the responsibility and wanted to spend more time practicing law, so I took over."

"Perhaps you could fill me in on exactly what the managing partner of a law firm does?" Charles asked. "I'm really woefully ignorant about the whole thing."

Royce nodded. It registered with Charles that Royce was quite a handsome man in a dignified sort of way with a tall, slim body and a full head of almost white hair. Charles pegged his age as being in the late forties, although he probably looked younger than his years.

"Basically, the managing partner is responsible for personnel decisions, the assignment of responsibilities, and the purchasing of the necessities for doing business."

"How many people work here?" Joanna asked.

"Right now, we're running with a lean staff. We have one junior partner, two associates, two paralegals, and five secretaries."

"Still, that's a lot of staff to keep track of on your own."

Royce smiled. "It isn't as complicated as it sounds. Harris and I each have a secretary. The other three are in a pool available to everyone. They do most of the work for the associates. The two paralegals float around wherever they're needed."

"Do the associates get to be partners some day?" Charles asked.

"After three years or so we evaluate their contributions to the firm and decide if they're bringing in enough business and serving a necessary function. If so, we offer that person the opportunity to become a junior partner."

"Does each senior partner work closely with one associate or the other?" Charles asked. "I'm just wondering if it's a mentoring sort of relationship."

"I suppose you could describe it that way. When a new lawyer joins, either Harris or I would take over their introduction to the firm. Teach him or her the ropes so to speak."

"How is that assignment arrived at?" asked Joanna.

"Well, it depends on interests and need. If we need someone to help me handle trusts and wills for instance, then we would first of all hire someone with a penchant for that, and I would mentor him or her."

"What was Harris's area of expertise?" Joanna asked.

"He handled some wills, as we all do working in a small town. But I suppose you would have to say that he primarily handled divorce law. He was very good at it."

Joanna shot me a quick glance.

"I would imagine that divorce lawyers make a lot of enemies. Angry spouses must often confuse the messenger with message," Charles said.

Jonathan Royce frowned. "It's not an area I would want to be in. We don't really handle criminal law here. We refer those cases to a more specialized firm, but I think that after criminal law, and perhaps injury claims, divorce is the most contentious. Spending hours listening to angry couples squabble is demoralizing, but somehow Harris did it and remained cheerful."

"He was divorced himself, however," Joanna pointed out.

"True. He got divorced from Dianna six months ago. But he continued to have a cordial relationship with his ex-wife."

"Did he have any enemies that you know of?"

Royce shrugged. "We were colleagues, but I don't know what might have been going on in his personal life. He was a tough competitor, but in the profession, he was generally well respected."

"Was he currently involved in any particularly contentious cases?"

"Sharon Thornby, the associate who worked with him, would be able to tell you that. Why don't I see if she's available?"

While he called, Charles sat there thinking the same thing he was pretty certain was also on Joanna's mind. If Harris turned out to be the killer shark of divorce lawyers in town, there could be a very long list of suspects.

Chapter Four

Sharon Thornby turned out to be painfully slender and extremely serious. Royce's secretary had taken them down a floor and into an office that looked south toward town rather than in the direction of Vermont. It was a fine office for someone starting out, but Charles was sure that every associate aspired to a spot on the third floor. Seniority in a law firm no doubt had its privileges in both salary and office location. In academe that was true as well, but the gradations in salary were very subtle. They were also not much discussed because college faculty were supposedly laboring solely to educate the young and for the sake of contributing to disinterested scholarship.

There was barely enough room for Joanna and Charles to sit side by side in front of Thornby's desk. She watched them maneuver their chairs around with a solemn expression on her face, as if they were there to hear the reading of a will and she was just waiting for the appropriate opportunity to express her condolences. When the condolences came, it was from the other side.

"We're very sorry for your loss," Joanna said, while Charles nodded in solemn agreement. "Had you worked for Mr. Harris very long?"

"Almost a year," Sharon Thornby replied.

It was difficult for Charles to tell if she was truly saddened by her boss's death or simply going through the formalities. He guessed that either by training or personality, she tended to suppress her emotions.

"What was he like to work for?" Joanna asked.

The young woman looked down at the blotter on her desk as if this were a question that might require more research.

"He was a highly skilled lawyer. I learned a great deal form him."

"Was he any fun?" Charles asked, trying to break the funereal mood.

She glanced at him as if to say that fun had nothing to do with the law.

"How had he seemed lately?" Joanna asked. "Was he particularly stressed or concerned about something?"

"What does any of that have to do with being killed in a mugging?" Sharon asked sharply.

"Well, we don't know for certain at this time that it was a mugging, so we have to consider every possibility," Joanna replied.

"You mean he might have been murdered?"

She's not strong on affect, but she can put two and two together, Charles thought.

"That is a possibility. So how did he seem lately?" Joanna persisted.

"The same as always. He was very organized and focused. I think that's why we got on well together. We didn't waste time with chitchat. We got right down to business."

"So he was rather intense?" Charles asked.

She nodded. "Most good lawyers are. When you have a case, you have to dig and dig, and then dig some more. He could be relentless, especially when he had a divorce case and was trying to ferret out where a spouse had hidden his assets."

Joanna nodded. "Did he have to do that often?"

"There are a surprising number of wealthy people in this corner of the state. When they get divorced, the person who worked for the money—often, but not always, the husband—is sometimes unwilling to split fairly with his spouse. He often tries to conceal the extent of his assets. Between ourselves and the forensic accountants we hire, we are generally successful in seeing that our client gets her fair share."

"Mr. Harris must have collected his fair share of enemies as well," Charles said.

She shrugged, "It goes with the territory." Then her eyes widened. "Do you think the spouse of a client killed him?"

"Seems like something to think about," Joanna said. "Have you had any recent cases where the spouse, male or female, went away mad?"

"The most recent ones have been pretty amicable. The last one that turned nasty was the Baniff case about three months ago."

"Who's Baniff?" Joanna asked.

"Lester Baniff was a tech wizard who moved out here after he graduated from MIT He created his own online company providing some type of cyber communication service to people running small businesses. He had an office right here in Opalsville. I went to the place once with Ray to interview him. He had married a woman named Laura who graduated from Opal College a few years ago, so I guess that's how he ended up out here. They had a pretty happy marriage for a while, but then Laura Baniff got fed up with him spending all his time working and pretty much ignoring her."

"Is that a common story?" Charles asked, thinking that he done something similar through much of his first marriage.

"Sure. The guy is ambitious. That's fine with the woman. After all, no one wants a lazy husband. But she thinks going into the marriage that once they make a pot of money, he'll slow down, they'll start a family, or at least they'll do some of the romantic things they've dreamed about but never had the time to do early on. Unfortunately, there isn't enough money or fame to satisfy him. He enjoys the work for its own sake, so he never does slow down. Then one day the wife wants to get off the train."

"Is that what happened with the Baniffs?" Joanna asked.

"Yes. After fifteen years of marriage, she was frustrated because they hadn't started a family, and he was hardly ever home. Of course, he said that he'd been working hard to provide her with all the material comforts she could want. Neither one of them was wrong, but they just weren't moving in the same direction."

"And he hid some of his wealth?" Joanna asked.

"He had a number of offshore accounts, but with the help of our accountant, we dug into his tax returns and found out the banks he was using. It ended up costing him a lot, and he was really angry about it. He came charging in here one day without an appointment and pretty much forced his way into Ray's office. Fortunately, Ray was a big guy, while Lester Baniff isn't. I guess he thought better of getting physical. He muttered a few threats and left."

"Did he threaten to kill Mr. Harris?"

"That was probably mixed in there somewhere with all the profanity, it usually is. But this was all settled over three months ago. I think Baniff paid what he had to and went back to work making millions more. Ray never mentioned hearing anything further from him."

What's the name of Baniff's business?" asked Joanna.

"BusServe."

She wrote it down in her notebook. "Any other threats to Mr. Harris that you know about?"

Sharon Thornby shook her head. "But like I said, I've only been here a year. Ray worked at the firm over twenty-five years and handled a lot of divorces in that time. But most people don't hold grudges, at least not against lawyers. They may resent the spouse every time they have to make out a support check or think about what they lost in the division of property, but the lawyer is usually out of sight and out of mind."

"How did he get along with his own ex-wife?" Charles asked.

"As I said, we pretty much confined our conversations to business. He wasn't one to discuss his personal life beyond sometimes mentioning what he'd done over the weekend. I've never met her or even heard anything about her."

They thanked Sharon Thornby and headed back to the car.

"I'm not sure that was very helpful," Joanna said. "All we got is the name of one guy who seemed to get the anger out of his system three months ago."

"Maybe so, but some people do hold grudges and act on them later."

She nodded. "I'll have a chat with Baniff and see what I find out. But I don't see Ray Harris agreeing to have dinner with him."

"I can understand a guy being angry when he builds up a business like that, and then loses a big chunk of money as the result of a divorce."

Joanna gave Charles a level glance. "When you're married, you're a team. She was providing emotional, physical, and possibly financial support for him all the time he was building up that business. She deserved her fair share."

He nodded. "I suppose you're right."

"Do you think much about your ex-husband?" Charles asked after a minute.

"Hardly ever. We were only married a little over a year. We had no children and no money. He already had a new girlfriend before we even split up. By the time we were divorced, he'd probably forgotten my name. If you looked under 'young and stupid' in the dictionary, there would be a picture of us grinning like idiots." She turned to look at him. "I know it's different when you're widowed, but do you think about Barbara much."

21

Charles considered the question. "We were married a long time and raised a daughter together. I frequently think about some of the things we did together, but most of all when I think about our marriage, I focus on all the mistakes I made. Things I don't want to do again with us, like make work a bigger priority than family."

Joanna grinned. "You don't work anymore, so that should be easy."

Charles shook his head. "Most healthy men can always find something else to spend their time on than family. It's the nature of the beast. Even when you're retired, you have to set priorities or things can get away from you."

Joanna reached over and gave his arm a squeeze.

"I'm sure you're more than capable of doing that, and anyway, I'll remind you."

Chapter Five

Charles had to hurry to get from the offices of Barlow, Harris, and Royce to the soup kitchen where he was due to work the lunch shift. The church hall had recently hired a woman as maintenance person, and she was extremely prompt and efficient. By the time Charles got down to the basement, she was already standing by the tables stacked along the wall, tapping her foot impatiently.

She gave Charles a thin smile. "I was getting ready to do it myself."

"Sorry, I got delayed."

She nodded and easily lifted her end of one of the heavy tables. Charles took the other, and they carried it into place where they began to set it up. The woman's name was Blossom, which to Charles's way of thinking was an inappropriate name for the strong, sturdy, laconic woman who somewhat intimidated him. But even if she did frighten him a bit, he had to admit that she did her job better than any of the maintenance men he had worked with in the past, and they quickly had the room properly arranged. Blossom took one final glance around to make sure all was in order, nodded to Charles, and then went off to perform other duties.

By this time, the women in the kitchen were marching out, ready to place the food on the table. Charles went to his usual assigned place at the end where he doled out the carb of the day. Today it was, as usual, mashed potatoes. The person who carried it into the dining room and took her accustomed place next to him was Karen Melrose, whom he had known since starting at the kitchen a couple of years ago. They had even gone out on one disastrous date, which had ended with Karen being shot when she stepped in front of Charles, the intended victim. He was surprised to see her because she had been away for a couple of weeks on her honeymoon.

"Did you have a good time?" Charles asked in a whisper, as the folks looking for food began to pour into the basement.

"It was wonderful," Karen gushed. "Harold is just so romantic."

Charles smiled wanly. His encounters with Harold Van Sant had always been rather fraught, starting with the very first one when

Harold had virtually challenged him to a duel because Van Sant thought he had insulted Karen. He was a very small man—Charles thought of him, uncharitably, as The Homunculus—but his emotions were those of a giant, so one had to proceed carefully with him. He was a clinical psychologist and had recently been working at the counseling center at the college. He had suffered a serious beating as part of a case Charles was involved in solving, and immediately upon his recovery, he and Karen had decided to marry, much to the chagrin of Karen's son and daughter

Karen and Charles served the food, having no opportunity to speak for the next twenty minutes. When the crowd was finally seated and enjoying their lunch, Charles turned back to her.

"How was Hawaii?"

"Marvelous. Of course, we spent much of the time in our hotel room," she replied with an arch look.

"Of course," Charles said soberly, hoping to avoid any intimate details of Karen's personal life that involved The Homunculus.

"Has anything been happening around here while we were away?"

Charles was about to reply in the negative, when he recalled last night's adventure.

"A man was murdered outside Chasborne's last night while I was there for my birthday party."

"Happy birthday," Karen said automatically, but then suddenly she frowned. "You didn't find another body, did you?"

Charles shrugged. "I didn't exactly find it; it sort of came to me while I was in the men's room. He staggered in and collapsed on the floor."

Karen gave a slightly hysterical giggle. "Perhaps I should have kept going out with you, Charles. At least life would never be dull."

"I'm sure it will never be dull with Harold either."

She gave him a wink. "At least not in some ways, although he doesn't have your nose for trouble."

"I wish I didn't have it either."

"Was this person the victim of a crime?"

Charles nodded

"Who was he?"

"An attorney here in town by the name of Raymond Harris."

24

"I've heard of him. He represented Harold's first wife during their divorce."

"Harold was married before?" Charles asked in surprise. He could hardly believe that one woman would marry Van Sant, now apparently there were two of them.

"Oh, yes. He was married to Sylvia for over twenty-five years. She's a therapist as well. They were partners in a practice. That's why Harold hates Ray Harris. As a result of the divorce, Harold had to give up the entire practice to Sylvia, and he had no money left to reestablish himself. That's why he's working at the college mental health clinic today."

"Where was Harold last night at around eight o'clock?" Charles asked.

Karen started to laugh, but it died on her lips when she saw that Charles was serious. "He was with me. We were both jetlagged and spent the evening at home. Anyway, the divorce was settled over five years ago. Why would Harold kill the lawyer now?"

That was a good point, and the same one that made Lester Baniff a less than perfect suspect.

"I suppose you're right," Charles said with an apologetic smile. "Sorry if I sounded like I was accusing Harold of anything."

"But you know who hated Harris even more than my husband is the new Dean of the School of Arts and Sciences at Opal College, Stanley Carson."

Charles had heard from his friend and head of the English Department, Yuri Abramovitch, that Stanley Carson, an historian specializing in nineteenth century British history, had been offered the position. It was not unusual for Opal College to promote one of their own from the faculty into the administration. But Charles had been surprised to hear that Carson, a very dedicated scholar who frequently published in good journals and presented at conferences, would want to make such a change. Being a dean was a demanding position time wise that would force him to drastically curtail his writing and research. It would be virtually a career change for him.

"Why does Carson hate Harris so much?" Charles asked.

"Apparently, he lost so much in his divorce settlement that in order to meet alimony and child support payments, he had to take the job as dean," Karen explained.

It was true that being a dean paid much better than even the rank of full professor that Carson had held, so perhaps Charles now had his explanation for why Stanley had made the change. He could well imagine that a person dedicated to scholarship would bitterly resent having to become an administrator due to a divorce settlement. Stanley Carson would definitely be someone for Joanna to pay attention to.

"When was his divorce?"

"I think Harold told me it was finalized about two weeks ago. Right around when the man became dean."

"Thanks for the information," Charles said.

"So is Harold off the hook?" Karen asked.

Charles smiled. "I can't speak for Joanna, but I'd say you've put a much more likely fish on the hook in his place."

"Thank goodness. I wouldn't want you going after Harold for murder. I know from experience, Charles, that you can be dogged."

"I prefer the word persistent."

Karen just gave him a look.

Chapter Six

Since the soup kitchen was about halfway between the college and his house, Charles decided to travel on to the college in hopes of seeing Yuri and getting more information about Stanley Carson. Yuri was an avid gossip and could be relied upon to know a great deal about any unsavory personal event being bruited about on campus.

It was a warm late August day, and Charles was glad that he hadn't eaten at the soup kitchen or he would have gotten drowsy on the trip north of town and up into the hills where the campus was located. As it was, he had grabbed an energy bar of uncertain age out of the glove compartment of his car and hoped that would sustain him until dinner. He parked in the lot next to the English building. Because he was a professor emeritus, he still had an office that he could use as he wished. In fact, it was the same office he'd worked out of for almost thirty years.

He climbed the two flights of stairs to the English Department and went to the right down a short hall to where Yuri was located. The door was ajar. Charles knocked. It was quickly pulled open, and Yuri stood there, his head of gray hair even more mussed than usual.

"Ah, Charles, good to see you. It will give me an excuse to take a break from the usual last-minute panic."

"Panic about what?"

"Ah, getting people to teach English composition. I've been on the phone all morning. As you know, none of the full-time faculty want or are required to teach it, so every year I must find enough part-time teachers desperate enough to cover the courses and willing to work for a pittance. I tell you Charles, this part of the job is a real pull."

Charles paused for a moment to translate Yuri's comment in his mind. Yuri was one of the world's most renowned interpreters of James Joyce, but his grasp of the American vernacular was uniquely his own. After an instant, Charles grasped that Yuri had meant it was a real drag.

Charles nodded. "It's also a shame that we exploit young scholars by paying them next to nothing and offering them little hope of future full-time employment. It makes you wonder whether there will be a next generation of scholars."

Yuri shrugged his shoulders. "It is what it was," he announced grandly.

"I wanted to ask you what you've heard about Stanley Carson taking over as dean. I gather that it has something to do with his recent divorce."

The delighted smile of the rabid gossip came over Yuri's face. Charles wondered if this was a habit he had developed in his youth while still living in the old Soviet Union, where the true news was usually passed along surreptitiously from one person to another.

"Indeed, it does. In fact, the position was almost guaranteed to Miles Barker in biology until Carson expressed interest. Since he had more influence with the administration, he landed the job."

"And it had something to do with his divorce?"

Yuri nodded. "The word is that he desperately needed the money as a result of his divorce settlement. Did you ever meet his ex-wife, Samantha?"

"No."

"Ah, she is one hot mommy, and at least ten years younger than Stanley. I've heard that he married later in life, and she had been his student when he taught down in Georgetown. That was all before he came to Opal, so I don't know the details. They have two children who must be in their early teens by now."

"Do you know why the marriage broke up?"

"Carson was always a bit of a dry twig, more given to scholarship than relating to people, although the more dedicated history students seem to respect him. From what I've heard, Samantha was getting it on with Clive Parker over in the romance languages department, and her husband found out about it. She refused to end the affair. Hence, the divorce."

"Parker? Are you sure?" Parker was a rather rotund fellow who always had a jolly smile. Charles wondered if he'd discovered the reason for the man's perpetual good cheer.

"I know, not much in the looks department, but he speaks fluent French," Yuri said with a broad wink.

"So Samantha was cheating on Stanley, but he's the one who got taken to the cleaners."

"From what I heard, her lawyer was a real barracuda. He went right for the femoral."

Charles thought Yuri probably meant the jugular but had to admit that the effect would be the same. Stanley Carson had ended up in a pool of metaphorical blood.

"I wonder who her lawyer was. I might be able to use him if I ever get sued for unfair labor practices," Yuri mused.

"You're too late. He was murdered last night." Charles explained the circumstances of Harris's death.

"Too bad. The bad ones always die young. Speaking of bad ones, you will be attending the reception kicking off the fundraising campaign for our new technology center tomorrow night, won't you? There will be quite a crowd of wealthy folks from all over the country who have ties to Opal."

"Of course not. I hated that sort of thing before I retired. Why would I go to one now?"

"Joanna is coming."

"How do you know?"

"I'm on the organizing committee, and I just received a list of those who have responded affirmatively."

"She must have forgotten to tell me."

"Well, you can't let a good-looking woman like Joanna wander around alone among all those wealthy guys or you might be needing a divorce lawyer yourself."

Charles gave him a sharp look.

"Just joking, of course, Charles. But you know what we say back in Mother Russia, a woman who can make good borscht is always in demand."

Charles couldn't even begin to figure that one out.

"I guess I'll be there," he said.

Chapter Seven

Charles and Joanna were sitting in the inglenook by their kitchen fireplace, each sipping a small scotch. Although it was far too warm to have a fire, they enjoyed sitting next to each other in what felt like a safe, secure place and sharing the news of the day's events. Charles had come to appreciate that these were the truly special times in married life. He wished he had shared more of them with his first wife, Barbara, and he wasn't about to miss out on them now. A pot of chili that he had made in the morning was staying hot in the slow cooker, and soon they would have a nice dinner together.

"Did you learn anything new about the Harris case after I left you this morning?" he asked, breaking the comfortable silence.

"Mostly negatives. Believe it or not, Chasborne's doesn't have any security camera outside, not even in their parking lot. So there was no luck there. I reviewed all the witness reports taken last night, and nobody saw anything except for the hostess who spotted Harris staggering in the front door."

"Is there any record of whom he was planning to have dinner with?"

"I checked with his secretary at the law firm, and she had nothing written down. We had already gone through his work computer, but he only used that for legal work and didn't keep a daily calendar there."

"What about his phone?"

"Disappeared. We searched his home and office with no success. He had a second computer at home. I have a tech person going through it, but so far, nothing."

"Where do you think his phone went?" asked Charles.

"We have to assume that the killer took it."

"You mean at the time Harris was attacked. Wouldn't he have struggled?"

"If someone walks up to you and stabs you in the heart, you'd probably go into shock almost immediately and fall down. If the killer had his wits about him, he could easily have gone thorough

Harris's pockets and grabbed his phone without meeting any resistance."

"So you think Harris was on the ground, and his killer thought it was all over and left."

She nodded. "He wouldn't have wanted to spend more time than he had to bending over his victim's body."

"But then Harris got back to his feet and went into the restaurant."

"It's not unheard of according to the doctor. People who've been shot or stabbed often take themselves into the emergency room."

"So it must have been someone who didn't present a threat that attacked him," Charles said. "If it was somebody Harris knew and was afraid of, he would have been ready to put up a fight."

"Sounds right to me," Joanna sighed. "That's all we've got so far, and it isn't much."

"I found out a couple of things almost by accident," Charles said, and he went on to recount what he had learned from Karen about Van Sant and Stanley Carson.

"I'm sure you'd like us to bring in Harold Van Sant and work him over with a rubber hose until he confesses," Joanna said with a smile.

Charles shook his head. "Even I have to reluctantly admit that he probably didn't do it. Why would he wait years to get his revenge? Van Sant is a hotheaded little guy. He'd have challenged Harris to a duel or something during the divorce process. And anyway, Harris was a big man. The Homunculus would have needed to bring along a stepladder to reach the guy's heart."

Joanna snorted. "Sometimes you're so politically incorrect I think you should have been a cop."

"Only when it comes to Van Sant. What do you think about Stanley Carson as a suspect?"

"He seems more promising since the divorce was only finalized two weeks ago. Still, I would have expected the attack to take place during the divorce process itself." Joanna paused. "Yuri was pretty sure that Samantha Carson was cheating on her husband?"

"Yeah. Yuri was convinced her affair was with Clive Parker, a professor of romance languages."

"Sounds sexy. What are they?"

"Not exactly my field. From what I can recall, they're the languages that have their roots in Latin. So that would be French, Spanish, Portuguese, Italian, and, I think, Romanian."

Joanna grinned. "So apparently he was a real smooth talker."

"According to Yuri, Samantha Carson is way out of Parker's league in terms of looks, so he must have had something else going for him."

"I think I'll set up an appointment to meet with Dean Carson. If he's willing, do you want to tag along? I always like to get your opinion of these academic types."

"I only know him in passing and by reputation, but I'd like to be there if he's amenable."

"I've arranged to interview Lester Baniff down at the station tomorrow morning. I'll have another officer sit in with me on that, but you can watch through the observation mirror if you'd be interested."

Charles agreed.

"There was something else I wanted to ask you about," Charles said a moment later. "Yuri asked me if I was going to the Opal College fundraising reception tomorrow night, and I said that I didn't plan to be there. Then he told me that you had already said you were going. I was kind of surprised that you hadn't told me."

"I received the invitation at work, and it was only addressed to me as chief of police. That's the kind of town political event that I really have to attend. Opal College is the biggest employer around here, so I have to show up. I know how you hate those events, so I just assumed I'd go alone."

"But you didn't mention it to me," Charles said, trying not to sound accusatory.

"I meant to, really I did, but then with your birthday and the murder right afterward, I forgot."

"That's okay, but I think I'll go with you. Yuri wants me to be there, and it might be more fun for you if we're together."

Joanna looked doubtful. "Well, if you're sure."

"What's the matter?"

"Wasn't it just last year that you got in an argument with someone at one of these fundraisers and created a scene?"

"We just had a frank exchange of ideas. He was a Wall Street banker and thought that there was no need for students to learn the humanities anymore. I pointed out to him that if he remembered anything he'd learned about the humanities in the time he'd been at Opal, he wouldn't have said that."

"That doesn't sound too bad."

Charles shrugged. "Voices may have been raised."

"Given that you seem to create trouble, why would Yuri want you there?"

"He missed that reception, and I guess—surprisingly—the gossip about it never reached him."

"But this time, since I'm there, you'll be on your best behavior?"

"Anything for you darling," I said, giving her a kiss on the neck.

"Okay, Mr. Romantic, let's go dig into that chili."

Chapter Eight

The next morning after Joanna had left for work, Charles cleaned up from breakfast and then went into his study. Since Lester Baniff wasn't due to be interviewed until ten o'clock, Charles had time to get some work done on his writing before heading to the station. Feeling that he had learned enough about creating ads to at least give it a try, Charles developed a simple one and sent it out into cyberspace. Charles knew that if he wanted his books to be read by anyone beyond friends and family, he had to master marketing, but it was still with some regret that he took time away from writing for self-promotion

Academics traditionally had a mixed attitude toward fame. Most of them craved it but didn't feel comfortable going out in search of it. If fame sought you out, that was perfectly appropriate, but if you went looking for it, you were somehow a traitor to a scholarly tradition of modesty. Charles didn't feel that such coyness would be of benefit to him in the world of mystery writing.

Having completed his first writing task of the morning, Charles turned his attention to the larger question of what his next book was going to be about. Since his first book had ended up being titled *Vengeance*, his publisher had suggested that they stick with one-word titles. Although Charles could see this from a marketing standpoint, he was finding the concept to be rather limiting, and he had struggled for several days to find a word around which he could build a plot. Perhaps because of the investigation of the last two days, the word *Betrayal* sprang into his mind. Both parties to a divorce probably felt betrayed in some way by their spouse and that undoubtedly was a powerful emotion. Holding that thought in mind, he began to brainstorm. After an hour of coming up with a list of possible topics and then winnowing it down, Charles felt that he could see a glimmer of what his next book would be like. And it conveniently came just as he had to leave for the police station.

• • • •

LESTER BANIFF WAS DRESSED in a T-shirt that gaped around his neck and khaki shorts that looked none too clean. But they went well with his sockless feet in scuffed sneakers. That might have been normal tech-wear for guys in their twenties, but for Baniff, who was well into his thirties, it made him look like a boy refusing to grow up into a man, a sort of Peter Pan of cyberspace. Charles suspected that high tech was a field filled with cases of prolonged adolescence. Not knowing Lester's ex-wife, he already felt sorry for her. It was hard to be the sole responsible adult in a marriage.

Baniff slouched in a chair at the opposite end of the table from Joanna and an officer in his early thirties whom Joanna introduced as Sergeant Talbot. Charles didn't know him, but he was good-looking with an intelligent face.

"Is it true that three months ago you divorced your wife, Laura Baniff?" Joanna asked.

"Yeah. Actually, she divorced me. That isn't illegal, is it?"

"Did a lawyer by the name of Raymond Harris represent your wife?"

"That's right. Between the two of them, they took me to the cleaners."

"I would imagine you were pretty angry about that, weren't you?"

"Who wouldn't be?"

"In fact, you were so angry that you marched into Attorney Harris's office and threatened him. Isn't that true?"

Baniff suddenly sat up straight in his chair and leaned across the table. Charles saw Sergeant Talbot tense as if ready to repel an attack.

"What about it? Any man would be angry at losing half of what he's worked for to a woman who never did anything but shop."

"Where were you on Wednesday night?" Joanna continued.

"I was at work, like I am most nights."

"Were there other people there?"

"I have a couple of part-time employees but they leave at five. I usually stay on until I've finished whatever project I'm working on."

"What time did you leave work on Wednesday?"

"Not until ten. I had something that I really wanted to complete."

"But you were alone from five until ten?"

A sulky look came over his face. "I'm not going to answer any more questions until you tell me what this is all about."

"Attorney Harris was murdered on Wednesday night at approximately eight o'clock."

"Well, it wasn't me. Sure, I wanted to kill him at the time of the divorce, but I've moved on." He gave a high-pitched laugh. "I'm not the kind of guy who holds a grudge."

"But you've got no one who can testify as to your whereabouts at eight o'clock on Wednesday night?"

"I told you no."

"Any phone calls?"

He shook his head. "But I was logged onto my computer at that time. So your tech guys can examine my machine and see that I was working on my office computer at eight. It's a desktop, and I never remove it from my office."

"Two of my officers will be at your place of business this afternoon at two o'clock to examine your computer."

"I'll even show them how to do it," Lester Baniff said with a smirk. "Can I go now?"

"Yes. Sergeant Talbot will see you out."

The two men left the room. A few seconds later, Joanna stuck her head in the doorway. "Did you believe him?"

"He's a hothead, and he had motive. But I'm not sure that I see Baniff doing it after all this time. I think all his planning skills go into his work."

"Yeah, neither do I. I got in touch with Dean Carson. He's willing to meet with us at four o'clock. Is that okay with you?"

"Fine. All I've got to do this afternoon is go to the gym."

"Chief?" a voice asked from out in the hall.

Joanna turned and motioned for Charles to join her in the hall.

"Charles, I'd like you to meet Sergeant Dave Talbot. He's just been promoted into the detective bureau. Dave, this is my husband, Charles Bentley."

"Congratulations on your promotion," Charles said, shaking his hand.

"It's great to meet you," the young man said with a warm smile. "You're sort of a legend around the department."

"Oh?"

"Yeah, whenever an officer stumbles on a piece of evidence by accident or a wild hunch pays off, we say that they've just done a Bentley."

Charles could see Joanna barely suppressing a smile.

"I see," Charles said.

"That's not a bad thing," Talbot went on, suddenly looking worried that he'd offended Charles. "It shows that you've got good—"

"Instincts," Charles said.

"That's right," the sergeant said, appearing relieved. "You've got good instincts."

"I'll show you out," Joanna said to Charles. Charles said goodbye to Talbot and walked out of the station with his wife.

"Why do I have the feeling he was going to say that I have good luck?" Charles asked.

"You've got that as well, Charles. As much as I hate to admit it, you do manage in some unique way to get results.

"I'll try to focus on the bright side that I'm a legend. After all, that can't be all bad, can it?"

"I'll see you at the dean's office at four. Bring along those famous instincts."

Chapter Nine

Charles had been a member of the Flight or Fight Gym for a bit over a year. Run by Jeff Cohen, who, rumor had it, had once been a Navy SEAL, it catered to those who were serious about staying in shape. Charles had first been given a detailed fitness test by Jeff that had resulted in the development of a routine appropriate to his age and physical condition. Every month, one of the staff members tested Charles's progress and tweaked the program so his muscles would continue—as they liked to say—to be surprised into making new developments. Charles often found a new routine to be more startling than surprising to his muscles. Overall, however, he had to admit that he was probably in the best shape he'd been in since his twenties. It was required that he show up at the gym three times a week. This meant that he had to carefully schedule his week so as to fit in his workouts. Whenever Charles found himself grumbling about having to do this, he would look around at the condition of other folks his own age and quickly decide to stick to his schedule. Growing old was not just a state of mind, but also a state of body. And a sane mind in a sound body was the motto he tried to follow.

Jeff Cohen was standing behind the counter talking with Holly, one of the trainers, when Charles entered the gym.

"Charles, can I see you in my office for a minute?" Jeff asked, breaking off his conversation with Holly.

Whenever Jeff called him into the office, Charles felt like he was being brought before the headmaster at the boarding school his father had sent him to. Nothing good could ever come of it. As he followed Jeff, he racked his brains trying to think of any infraction he might have been guilty of, but it seemed to him that he had been the model gym member.

"Have a seat," Jeff said, gesturing toward the chair in front of his desk. "And stop looking so apprehensive, you haven't done anything wrong, at least not that I know about. I want to talk with you about Ray Harris."

"Did you know him?"

"He was a member here, and we've had a number of conversations over the years. He was in the Army for a while before he went to law school, so we had something in common."

"Well, I can't tell you much about his death. First of all, it's privileged information, and second, the police don't know a lot yet."

"Actually, I think there are some things I may be able to tell you that you can pass on to Joanna."

Charles sat quietly and waited. Jeff wasn't somebody to be rushed.

"Ray was a man with a mission," Jeff said. "He wasn't just a highly aggressive divorce lawyer, but one who usually represented women. From what he hinted at to me one time, his mother had been divorced and cheated rather badly by the terms of the settlement. So when Ray became a lawyer, he was determined to see that other women would get a better deal. Like most guys on a mission, he may have gone too far sometimes. He made a lot of enemies, but he was a pretty fearless person. People who are committed to something don't always weigh the risks."

"Are there any enemies in particular that you're thinking of?"

"There was one that seemed to even give Harris pause. A man named Chandler Wright."

"I don't recognize the name."

"He's not a local. He's a real estate developer from down in Manhattan. But he and his wife, Clarissa, built a summer cottage up here, more of a mansion actually. Anyway, I guess there was trouble in paradise, and Clarissa left Chandler in Manhattan and moved into the summer place. She sued for divorce and hired Ray to represent her. I guess it was a pretty acrimonious divorce, and surprisingly, Ray proved to be more than a match for the battery of big city lawyers Wright hired. Clarissa got a great settlement. According to Ray, Chandler Wright was furious and threatened to destroy him."

"When did all this happen?"

"I think it was about two years ago."

That would be before Sharon Talbot came on board, Charles thought, *and that would explain why she hadn't mentioned it.*

"So do you think this Chandler Wright killed Ray? Two years is a long time to wait to get revenge."

Jeff shrugged. "The worst enemies to have are patient ones. But I think Wright is more the kind of guy who would destroy your business rather than murder you. Ray mentioned to me that the firm had lost a few important clients over the last couple of years due to Wright's influence. Course it could be that I'm wrong. Maybe Wright's patience ran out and he finally hired someone to kill Ray. He certainly has enough money that he wouldn't have to get his own hands dirty."

"I'm not sure how Joanna will want to proceed on this information," Charles said.

"Yeah, Wright is probably a tough nut, but a chat with Clarissa, his ex-wife, might prove helpful. She would probably be willing to do anything she could to bring Harris's killer to justice."

Charles left Jeff's office and headed onto the gym floor to begin his workout thinking that this case had more layers than an onion.

• • • •

LOIS MICHAELS, THE dean's secretary, gave a big smile as he and Joanna entered the office. Although she was currently dating Yuri, Charles suspected that Lois had been somewhat interested in him a couple of years ago before he'd met Joanna. She was an attractive, full-figured woman who liked to laugh, an interesting contrast with the thin, saturnine Yuri. Charles suspected that she served to balance him, much as Joanna tended to offset his own more cerebral tendencies. Lois had been a guest at their Thanksgiving celebration and had proved to be the life of the party.

"Dean Carson will be with you in a couple of minutes," Lois said. "How have you both been?"

Joanna and Charles just had time to assure her that they were both well, when Carson stepped out of his office and invited them inside. He was a short, stocky man, mostly bald, but he carried himself with force and vigor. He appeared to be in his early fifties. The vanity wall that the previous dean had established behind his desk had disappeared, replaced by a Turner seascape. That alone gave the office a simple elegance it had lacked before.

"I gather you wanted to talk to me concerning the death of Raymond Harris," Carson said, once they were settled into chairs in front of his desk. Charles noticed that they weren't using the more casual conversational area near a window. Probably Carson wasn't expecting this discussion to be much fun.

"Yes, we're aware that Harris represented your wife during your divorce. We were wondering what your impression was of the man," Joanna said.

"Well, my opinion of the man is hardly objective. In his favor I will say that he effectively represented Samantha. I wish that he had been my lawyer rather than hers. Even though she was in the wrong, having carried on an affair for some time behind my back with another faculty member, Harris managed to portray me as a cruel and unfeeling man who didn't deserve to have custody of his children and should now have to pay a considerable amount monthly in spousal support."

"You must have been very angry at the time?" Joanna said.

"To be honest, I'm still angry, particularly at Samantha. I couldn't believe that she allowed her lawyer to so mischaracterize me. Now I only get to see my children on weekends twice a month and have minimal say in how she raises them."

"When was the last time you saw Harris?" Charles asked.

"When the divorce was finalized." He gave a wry smile. "Exactly a month ago today."

"Where were you this past Wednesday evening at eight o'clock?" asked Joanna.

"Where I am every evening, home working in my study on my research. I was in the midst of a book on the effects of the Corn Laws on nineteenth century British society when I had to take this job in order to cover my alimony and child support payments. I may have become an administrator out of necessity, but my passion is still for history. I refuse to abandon it. The life of the mind is something that Samantha never understood. She thought that I was being cold and unfeeling by locking myself up in my study every evening. But scholarship and teaching are my life. My mistake was in expecting her to understand that. Surely this was true for you as well, Charles, at least when you were at my time of life."

Charles nodded. "Although I have to say that, in retrospect, perhaps I was wrong not to have pursued a more balanced life."

Carson sighed. "I guess that's what I've learned as well. Now I have plenty of time in the evening for reading and writing because that's just about all I have to do."

"Is there anyone who could provide you with an alibi for Wednesday evening?" Joanna asked.

"I'm afraid not. I was alone, as I usually am. But I can assure you, for what it's worth, that I did not kill Raymond Harris. He was merely an instrument of my wife's actions and not the cause."

As Charles and Joanna left the building, Charles said, "If Samantha Carson turns up dead, I think you know who to pick up right away."

"Yes. But I'm not so sure that I see him killing Ray Harris. Plus, he seems sadder and more beaten down than angry."

"His whole world has been turned around, and although he's managed to cope with the financial ramifications, I think he's still struggling with the emotional ones."

"It must have been painful for you hearing that, since it was so similar to what happened between you and Barbara toward the end. I'm sorry I asked you along. I wouldn't have if I'd known how the conversation was going to go."

"In looking back, I was rather like Carson, dedicated to teaching and scholarship at the expense of my family. I suppose I was a bit better off because Barbara kept her affair more discreet, and she died long before it was discovered. I loved Barbara and love Amy, as I'm sure Stan loved Samantha and still loves his children, but we'd both become infatuated with a vision of the ideal intellectual life when we were young, long before we had our families. And it was too late for us to change once we married. As Flaubert said, "The man is nothing, the work—all.'"

"Not the recipe for a happy life."

"No."

Joanna reached over and took his hand. "Do you regret giving all that up for what we have?"

Charles gave her hand a squeeze. "Never think that for a moment."

Chapter Ten

Charles was wearing a suit for the second time in a week. This time, however, Joanna was not in uniform. She was wearing a black sheath that showed off her figure to good effect, and he could see that several sets of aging academic eyes were following her around the room at the fundraising reception.

The reception was being held in the grand rotunda of what was once the main library. In the middle of the twentieth century, the building had been converted into administrative offices, but the large open lobby had remained intact, and it was often used when the need arose to impress visitors. Tables laden with finger foods and drinks were located along the curved walls, and students masqueraded as service staff, picking up empty glasses and discarded plates and placing them in the trash. The crowd was made up of distinguished members of the local community, higher administrators, selected faculty, and alumni both important and self-important. The alumni were the real target of the event because shortly after the night was over, they would find themselves being solicited to increase what was probably an already sizable contribution to the collage.

The only pleasant part of the event for Charles was bumping into the occasional former student and discovering what they had been doing in the decades since they had left. Although the audience heavily gravitated toward those who had achieved substantial financial success, Charles was often surprised to find that even some of those who majored in English had managed to parlay their degree into a comfortable life.

After about an hour, Charles's feet had begun to ache from standing on the marble mosaic floor, and he felt a slight headache coming on from having consumed too much inexpensive champagne. He spotted Joanna deep in conversation with a crowd of men who seemed to find her a source of fascination. Attractive women always were a bright, shiny object to middle-aged men, but one who daily carried a gun seemed to add a sexual frisson that was especially exciting for them. He was about to walk along the edge of the room and rescue her, not that she seemed like she needed it, when a voice brought him up short.

"Who are you and what do you do here?" someone asked in a deep bass.

Charles turned to his right. A fat man was leaning against the wall as if he needed its substance to prop him up. When Charles stopped to look at him, he pushed himself away from the wall and took a step forward, invading Charles's personal space with his protruding belly.

"I'm Charles Bentley, a retired professor."

"What did you teach?" the man asked in a wheezing voice. Charles thought he detected a Texas drawl.

"English."

The man gave an abrupt laugh. "Is there good hunting around here?"

"I wouldn't know. I don't hunt."

"Of course not, you've probably never held a firearm in your life."

"Not since I got back from Vietnam."

The man's eyes peered out more sharply from the folds of his chubby face.

"I used to be president of Stanton Corporation. You've heard of us?"

"An arms merchant, am I right?"

"Don't say it like that. The stuff we provided probably kept you from getting your ass blown away over there."

Charles smiled. "Did you serve as well?"

The man glared. "I was defending the home front."

Charles nodded and turned to walk away, but the man wasn't done.

"I can't carry a weapon in this state, but if we were back home, I'd have a gun on my right hip. If I reached for it with bad intent, what would you do Mr. English Professor who hates guns?"

Charles turned back as the man walked closer, his right hand reaching for his waist and his protruding stomach almost touching Charles's. Charles's right hand went into his front pocket, and in a smooth motion, he flipped open a short knife with his thumb and poked the point of the blade into the man's soft abdomen.

"You'd never reach that weapon because you'd need your right hand to hold in your intestines."

The fat man blinked and took an involuntary step backward, but Charles moved forward keeping the point of the knife up against him

A firm hand grabbed his right arm.

"There's someone I'd like you to meet, Charles," Joanna said very brightly, dragging him away. Charles quickly folded up the knife and returned it to his pocket.

"Was that a knife I saw?" she asked

"It's under three inches. Legal to carry."

"But not to poke someone in the stomach with."

"I was just showing him my knife. We were having a rhetorical discussion about bringing a knife to a gunfight."

"It looked more like assault to me."

Charles shrugged. "I didn't like him much."

"Every kid I arrest for assault says that. You don't usually attack people you like. What am I going to do with you, Charles?"

"Keep me away from fundraisers."

"I think I'm going to have to keep you away from other people."

"Only the ones like him."

Chapter Eleven

After Joanna went into work the next morning, after giving Charles a particularly long look and the admonition to behave himself, he settled down in his study and began to structure his new novel, tentatively titled *Betrayed.* After an hour, he had a sketchy outline of the first quarter of the book and a pretty good idea of how he wanted the first chapter to sound. He began writing the first chapter, hoping that by getting the tone right, he'd be inspired as to how he wanted the story to proceed. He didn't have any other obligations today. It wasn't his day for the soup kitchen or the gym, so theoretically he could spend all day writing. But Charles knew that his stamina would give out around lunch, and it would be best if he found some outside activity for the early afternoon. That way when he came back to prepare dinner, he would have renewed enthusiasm to carefully look over what he had written that morning.

Charles made himself a light lunch and decided that he would visit his daughter, Amy, at the art gallery downtown. He took his car so if he decided to continue on to the college, he'd have it with him. Fifteen minutes later, he'd parked in the municipal lot and had walked the three blocks to the gallery owned by Sanjay where Amy worked. A bell over the door rang as he stepped inside, and Amy looked up from where she stood reading at the counter.

"Hi, Dad," she said, coming around the counter and giving him a hug. "What have you been up to?"

"Oh, you know, this and that."

She eyed him shrewdly. "Have you been helping Joanna with the Harris murder case?"

"I wouldn't say *help*, I've just been tagging along." Charles glanced around the gallery. "Sanjay isn't here?"

"He's out making a delivery and don't try to change the subject. I'm sure you're more involved in this murder investigation than you're letting on."

Charles shrugged.

"You know, the dead man's wife, Dianna Harris, is one of our customers."

"Oh, for how long?"

"She's been coming in since Sanjay opened the shop, so a little over a year. Her husband came in with her at first, but for the last six months or so she's either been by herself or with Mona Royce. I think she's the wife of another lawyer at the firm."

"The Harrises got divorced six months ago, so that's probably why they don't come in together anymore."

"I didn't know that. But she's not the type to talk about her personal business or trash a former husband."

"What type is she?" Charles asked.

"I'd say she's smart and sophisticated. She has excellent taste in art and knows quite a bit about it, especially modern art."

"How about Mona Royce? I know her husband from the college and from looking into Harris's death. What's his wife like?"

Amy paused to think. "When the two of them are here together, I'd say Dianna Harris is definitely the dominant of the two. Mona comes across as more unfocused and definitely the less worldly. She also dresses in a much dowdier way than Dianna. It's a bit hard to see what they have in common, aside from their husbands working together."

"Quite often, friendships aren't really equal power relationships. One is dominant and one submissive."

"Doesn't sound ideal to me."

"We both know that relationships often aren't." Charles paused. "Speaking of relationships, have you and Sanjay set a date for your wedding yet?"

"I'd do it next week if it were up to me. When it's your second marriage, you aren't as patient with all the hoopla. The problem, as you might expect, is with Sanjay's parents, his mother in particular. Both of his brothers had rather large, traditional Indian weddings, and Sanjay is doing a lot of negotiating to get his mother to agree to something less elaborate for us. He says he's making progress, but it seems to be going along very slowly. I have a feeling we won't be tying the knot until the late spring next year."

"That's a nice time here in the Berkshires."

"We may have to go somewhere with an Indian temple, so who knows where it will be. I just know that I'm not going to ride in on an elephant."

"That would be worthy of a photo."

"Not one you'd like to see."

Charles gave Amy a hug, urged her not to worry, and to send his best to Sanjay. He promised to be in touch in the near future to set up a date for them to come over for dinner with Joanna and himself.

Charles walked back to his car and headed out to the college. He was thinking that perhaps he and Joanna should have a chat with Dianna Harris. As Harris's ex-wife, she would probably be aware of who his enemies, if any, might be. It will also give them a chance to determine if she might have a grievance against him. After all, they only had Royce's word that the split had been amicable. He parked in his usual spot and went up the stairs to the English Department office. After pulling the mail from the box, he went down the hall to his office. There were several handouts for on-campus events that Charles doubted he'd attend. A few were brochures for textbooks that he'd never use, and one or two were notices about conferences he had no intention of attending.

When he'd disposed of all that in his wastebasket, feeling a great sense of liberation, he sat back behind his desk and gazed out the window at the distant hills, looking very green and ripe in their late summer splendor. Soon those same hills would be a blaze of fall colors, then to be followed by the white mantle of winter. He wondered whether Joanna would be able to get a week off this winter. Last year, her first as chief of police, had been a hectic one with the death of an officer and the need to make some structural changes in the department. He hoped that they'd get a chance to take a belated honeymoon sometime this winter. He thought that they both, but particularly Joanna, needed a little change in routine.

There was a knock on the door. Charles walked across the office and pulled open the door, expecting to see Yuri's attenuated frame. The body that filled the doorway was definitely not Yuri's. It belonged to a very pretty blonde woman in her midthirties, who gave Charles a rather fetching smile and put out a slender hand.

"Hello, Professor Bentley, I'm Samantha Carson. May I speak with you for a few minutes?"

Charles nodded, too surprised to speak. He backed into his office and indicated that she should take a chair in front of his desk. She settled into the chair and crossed one shapely leg over the other. Although she was very slender and didn't have overtly obvious physical charms, she had a sensuous way about her that got a person thinking, as Yuri liked to say.

"How did you know I would be here?" Charles asked.

"Oh, I called the English office and the secretary told me you usually came in around this time."

Charles thought for a moment and realized that it was indeed true that he often showed up in this office on this day at this time. Even though he no longer had a schedule to adhere to, he had created one of his own that he followed quite religiously. There must be some comfort about following a habitual routine that caused us to have one even when it was unnecessary.

"How can I help you?" Charles asked.

"I gather from my former husband that you and your wife are investigating the murder of Ray Harris."

"My wife is the investigating officer. I was just along as an unofficial consultant."

"No matter." She paused for a moment and a strong emotion passed over her face. "I just want to be sure that you are taking his murder seriously. He was a good man, and his killer deserves to be brought to justice."

"Let me assure you that Chief Thorndike will put all the resources available to her into finding Harris's killer. Is your positive opinion of him based on how he handled your divorce?"

"Not that alone."

Charles waited.

"We were a couple for a while."

"I thought it was you and—"

She grinned. "Clive Parker. Well, it was for a while, but once the divorce proceedings started, I was seeing a lot of Ray. One thing sort of led to the other. When a man comes along and says that he's going to take care of you when you're going through a difficult time, you can form a strong attachment to him."

"Did your husband know that Ray was more than just your lawyer?" Charles asked.

"I don't think so, and even if he had, I can't see him attacking Ray. After all, he knew about Clive and me and never went after him. I don't think my husband cared what I was up to. He cared about his career first, and his children a distant second. I doubt that I even made the list. What got him upset was the divorce settlement and having to take the dean's job to pay the child support and alimony. That forced him to give up his precious teaching and research."

"That might be enough of a motive for him to kill."

She shook her head and smiled prettily. "Stan isn't a passionate man. He may be angry at the way the divorce turned out, but he'll just put his nose to the grindstone and cope. He isn't the type to attack Ray or me, for that matter."

"Okay. So you really don't have anything to contribute to the investigation?" Charles was getting tired of this self-centered woman, who seemed to have come into his office only to brag about her affair with Harris.

She gave him a pouty look. "I'm just trying to tell you that if Ray got involved with me, then maybe he did the same thing with some of his other clients. So there could have been other men who had it in for him." She stood up and stretched her arms over her head, showing off her slender figure. "What do you think?" she asked.

Charles wasn't sure whether she was asking him about her view of the murder investigation or her body.

"I'll pass it on to Chief Thorndike, and we'll take it under consideration."

Samantha gave him a dissatisfied look and sashayed out of the office. Charles watched her go thinking how fortunate it was that he had never married a student.

Deciding that it was time to leave before he got another unexpected visitor, Charles locked up his office and headed down the hall. As he walked past the English Department office, Yuri happened to step out into the hall.

"Ah, Charles, just the man I was looking for. President Dawson and I were talking about you earlier this morning. Were your ears aflame?"

"Not really," Charles said with a feeling of dread. Although he got on well with the president of Opal College, Charles knew it was never good to be the topic of conversation with administrators.

"Travis Merriman just gave a half-million dollars to the fundraising appeal, and he said it was all because of meeting you."

"Who is Travis Merriman?"

"A Texas industrialist. You'd remember if you saw him; he is a man of impressive girth. He said he spoke to you last night at the reception."

"Now I remember, we exchanged a few words."

"Well, they must have been the right words because he was very impressed with you. He told the president that Opal needed more men of direct action like yourself." Yuri paused with a puzzled expression. "Do you have any idea what he meant by that?"

"Not a clue," Charles replied.

Yuri shrugged. "In any event, President Dawson has directed me to invite you to attend every fundraising event we have from now on. Dawson said that he would be particularly looking for you."

Charles sighed.

Yuri patted him on the shoulder. "You know what they say, Charles, no good deed goes unpunished."

"Apparently, no bad deed either," Charles said, heading off down the hall.

* * * *

THAT NIGHT BEFORE DINNER, Charles and Joanna sat in the inglenook going over the day's events. Charles usually let Joanna go first because she had more to recount and he knew she appreciated having the opportunity to vent. When she was done, he told her about his conversation with Yuri. She began to laugh so hard that she almost choked on her drink.

"Let that be a lesson to you, Charles, not to make an impression on people."

"I was trying to make a bad one, but apparently it backfired."

"You should have guessed that intimidating a bully like that might make him a friend. People like that only respect force."

"I suppose I should have just slunk off like the weak-kneed English professor he had me pegged for being."

"I don't think you're capable of doing that," Joanna said, patting is hand. "I can't approve of your pulling a knife, but you had to stand up for yourself. It's just too bad that you'll have to attend more fundraisers. Now I'll have to assign an officer to accompany you around the room so you don't get involved in any other altercations."

"I've learned my lesson. I'll keep my mouth shut and look harmless."

"I don't think you can carry it off."

"Stanley Carson's ex-wife paid me a visit today."

Joanna gave him a level look. "Would that be the luscious Samantha? I hope you didn't practice any romance languages on her."

"I was the perfect gentleman."

"Hmm. What did she want?"

"Actually, she thought she had some information that might help us solve the Ray Harris murder."

"Oh, really. Are you sure she didn't stop by looking for a replacement lover for Clive whatever his name is?"

"Parker. Apparently, he had already been replaced by Harris."

"She was having an affair with Ray Harris?" Joanna said in surprise.

"So she claims. She suggested that maybe Ray made a habit of consoling women whose marriages were on the rocks in a way that went beyond the normal attorney-client relationship."

"Sounds exploitative."

"Maybe so, but clearly Samantha didn't feel that way. I'd say she was pretty broken up about Ray's murder and thought that if we knew about his behavior, it might give some new ideas for suspects."

"You mean like the husbands of every woman he's ever represented in a divorce."

"At least recently."

"Well, we can eliminate Lester Baniff. My people checked out his computer, and he was working on it at the time Harris was murdered."

"And Samantha doesn't think Stanley Carson cared enough about her to get physical with Ray. I think she's probably right."

"So who's left?"

"Chandler Wright is still in the picture. Of course, that divorce was two years ago, but according to Jeff Cohen, Wright has done some damage to the law firm's business. So it sounds to me like he still holds a grudge."

"I'd still prefer something more recent," Joanna said. "To stab someone in public like that suggests to me a high level of desperation. Sharon Thornby wasn't able to help us much, but maybe the other important woman in his life might be able to," Joanna said.

"You mean his ex-wife, Dianna Harris?"

Joanna nodded. "They've only been divorced for six months. Depending on how much he discussed work with her, she might have some suggestions for suspects. Also, she would know if he had any enemies in his personal life. I'm going to set up a visit with her tomorrow."

"Amy knows her. Apparently, she purchased a number of paintings at the gallery."

"Would you like to come along for the interview? You could use your masculine charm to get her to open up, just like you did with Samantha Carson."

"I was completely innocent."

"Do you know how often I hear that in the course of a day?"

"I'm telling the truth."

Joanna smiled. "I hear that a lot too."

Chapter Twelve

Charles sat in his study the next morning and thought about the different types of betrayal. Since *Betrayed* was going to be the title of his next book, he figured that he should have a plot and subplot that dealt with the same subject but from different angles. Several types of betrayal sprang to mind. There was the obvious betrayal of someone you loved by being unfaithful. There was betraying a friend by not helping him in a time of need. There was betraying those that you were sworn to care for and protect, such as the failure to fulfill one's obligations on the part of a doctor, a lawyer, a clergyman, or a police officer. Subtler, perhaps, was the betrayal of yourself, when you didn't live up to the values you claimed to hold dear.

Charles allowed his mind to gently mull over all of these. He found that by not forcing his ideas at this early stage of writing, plot points would often fall into place as if by magic. He suspected that on some unconscious level his mind was digesting the material and would reveal the answers to him at the appropriate time. The more he wrote fiction, the more convinced he was that we only know the surface of our minds, and most of the real activity lies deep in some portion of our brain that is inaccessible to our reason. *Many of our best ideas simply come to us*, he thought, *and they have us more than we have them.* Charles was more and more inclined to believe that the ancient writers who talked of being inspired by a muse were right on target.

The phone rang. It was Joanna informing him that she had made contact with Dianna Harris and that the woman would be able to meet with them a one o'clock. Charles volunteered to come to the police station so they could continue north from there to Harris's home. After hanging up the phone, Charles realized that it would be best if he headed directly out to the gym. This was the day for his workout, and he should fit it in during the morning when he had more energy.

So he got into his gym clothes and drove out to the Flight or Fight Gym. After his usual workout of about an hour, he returned home and had a light lunch. There was nothing like physical exhaustion to curb the appetite. Fifteen minutes later he was on his way to the police station. He waited only five minutes before Joanna came to collect him from the waiting room, and they took her car for the trip to the northern part of town.

"What did Amy tell you about Dianna Harris?" Joanna asked, as she turned left at the center of town.

"Not very much. Just that she thought Harris knew quite a lot about art and that she seemed intelligent and sophisticated. Oh, and she also said that Dianna is friends with Mona Royce, that's Jonathan Royce's wife. They would sometimes come into the gallery together."

"Two art lovers?"

"At least two women with enough disposable income to purchase art."

Joanna smiled. "You sound cynical."

"No, but lots of people buy art as part of a home decoration project without having any appreciation for art as art."

"I suppose that's true. I imagine that's what I would do."

They drove on in comfortable silence for another five minutes before turning off on a side road that led up into the hills. Charles was just starting to wonder whether they had taken a wrong turn, when they crested a hill and on the other side was a rural mailbox with Dianna Harris's address on it. A driveway led up an incline to a ranch home situated on the top of a low hill, which featured a sweeping view of the countryside.

"Must be money in helping folks get divorced," Joanna said.

"But apparently Harris didn't have the same killer approach to his ex-wife as he had to the husbands of his clients, or he'd have been the one living in this house and his wife would be in a small condo back in town."

When they rang the bell, a slender petite woman with dark brown hair, who gave them a pleasant but reserved smile, opened the door.

"You must be Chief Thorndike?" she said.

Joanna introduced herself and Charles, and the woman directed them to a sunroom in the back of the house that looked south in the direction of the Opal College campus. Charles thought he could see the spire of the old college chapel in the distance.

"You wanted to speak with me about my former husband?" Harris asked, once everyone was seated and had refused refreshments.

"First of all, let us express our condolences on your loss," Joanna said.

Dianna Harris nodded. "I'm still very upset over Ray's death. In many ways, he was a good man, one of a kind, actually. When we got divorced, he went out of his way to be generous to me. As a skilled divorce lawyer, he could have fought much harder to keep more of his money. But he didn't."

"Why do you think that was?" asked Joanna.

"I'm sure it was because he felt guilty."

"About what?"

"Being repeatedly unfaithful to me." She gave a small smile. "Look, in a way, Ray was a victim of his own best impulses. He fought very hard for his clients, who were usually women being taken advantage of by their unscrupulous husbands. He was a romantic and in his own mind he was riding in on a white charger to protect these women. I'm sure some of the women saw him that way as well. One thing frequently led to another, and Ray became romantically involved with several of his clients."

"When did you find out about it?" asked Joanna.

"I ran into Chandler Wright at a party in town, and he took great delight in telling me that Ray had been having an affair with his wife, Clarissa. I didn't believe him at first, although why I didn't, I don't know. After all, I first met Ray when I got divorced from my first husband, and we were involved almost from the start. I guess I thought that because he married me, what we had was special. But apparently, he couldn't resist getting close to many of his clients. He had a tendency to fall in love easily but superficially."

"Did you ask Clarissa Wright about it?"

"No. I asked Ray, and after hemming and hawing for a bit, he at least had the decency not to deny it." She gave a small sigh. "That was the end of us. Ray was too busy playing the hero to be a faithful husband, and I couldn't tolerate that. We never had any children, so I thought it was best to draw a line under it."

"I thought Chandler Wright lived in Manhattan and that his wife got the summer place in Opalsville? How did you happen to run into him?" Charles asked.

"His permanent residence is in Manhattan, but he's very involved in some local charities and the community theater up here. He comes up for a few days almost every month in the good weather. You always see him around. I think he stays at the Opalsville Inn now that his wife has the house."

"Did Ray ever mention anything about Wright threatening him?" Joanna asked.

She shook her head. "Ray didn't discuss his work with me. Do you think Wright killed him?"

"We have no evidence that he did. But there are indications that he may have been trying to harm the law firm by taking away business."

"Mona Royce mentioned to me that her husband was concerned about that." Dianna paused. "I don't know whether I should tell you this because it's probably not relevant, but Mona was giving serious thought to divorcing Jonathan."

"Do you know why?" Joanna asked.

"I think she just feels badly neglected. Mona is a rather dependent person, and she really relies on Jonathan for her sense of who she is. I think that recently she's felt that he just cares about work. She asked me to talk to Ray about representing her in a divorce. But when I asked Ray, he said he wouldn't do it. It might not strictly speaking be unethical, but he said it would make him very uncomfortable to be opposing another partner in the firm. He gave me the names of a couple of other divorce lawyers to pass on to her. I did that, but I haven't heard any more about it from Mona. It might have just been a passing fancy for her. It's hard to imagine her without Jonathan."

Joanna and Charles stood, ready to leave, but Dianna remained seated.

"I don't want to give you the wrong impression about Ray. From the outside, one could easily see his behavior as preying on vulnerable women, but I doubt that the women saw it that way. I know I didn't when he represented me. If he hadn't married me, I would have gone on my merry way after our affair with very kind thoughts about Ray as a caring, supportive person."

"And you don't know of any enemies he's mentioned recently."

"Aside from Chandler Wright, I can't think of anyone."

Joanna and Charles thanked Dianna Harris and left.

"What did you make of all that?" Charles asked as they walked to the car.

"I want to have a talk with Clarissa Wright. I need to find out if Dianna Harris is correct, and that Ray was having an affair with Clarissa." She pulled out her cell phone, walked a few feet away, and began making calls, while Charles looked admiringly at the hills surrounding them.

This is certainly a grand location, he thought. *It might be a bit treacherous getting up the hills in the winter, but with a four-wheel drive, it would easily be doable.*

"Where are we going?" he asked Joanna as she walked back to the car.

"To visit Clarissa Wright. I just gave her a call, and she'll see us now. She lives just two miles further north."

"Are you thinking that Chandler Wright looks like our prime suspect at the moment?"

"He had motive, and since he's been hanging around Opalsville, he had opportunity."

"But I can't imagine Harris being willing to have dinner with him," Charles objected.

"Maybe Wright had someone else call Harris and make the appointment. Wright could certainly have paid someone to pretend to be a woman in distress and arrange to meet Harris for dinner. It sounds to me like Harris would have been happy to keep such a date."

"So it was all a setup?"

Joanna shrugged. "It's going to be hard to prove. That's why I want to talk to the wife."

About five minutes later, they pulled up in front of a log cabin. Not the rustic type that had housed Daniel Boone or Davy Crockett, but more a mansion built out of logs with a sweeping porch all along the front and a full second floor. Joanne knocked on the door. A tall, elegant blonde in her midthirties dressed in tight designer jeans and a silk blouse answered.

"Mrs. Wright?" Joanna asked.

"Actually, I go by Clarissa Stevens, my professional name. I never changed it when I married Chandler. Just as well since I don't have to go to the problem of changing it back now," she said with a wry smile.

She directed them to a large room off to the right that was dominated by a fireplace almost large enough to walk into. Charles had only seen ones the size of this in early colonial reproduction homes in the eastern part of the state. The colonists had cooked in them. Charles couldn't picture this woman doing the same.

"What was your profession before you married?" Charles asked.

"I was a fashion model."

"Is that how you met your husband?"

"Indirectly. I traveled all over the world, but my home base was in Manhattan. I met Chandler at a party given by a rich person who invited some models and actors to give the event some glamour."

"And Chandler Wright swept you off your feet?" Charles asked.

"Hardly. But he was very attentive and obviously attracted to me."

"Is that why you married him?"

She smiled. "It's always flattering to be admired by a wealthy, powerful man. But I am above all a realist, Mr. Bentley. I was getting to an age when the job offers were starting to slow down, and I was no longer as much in demand. I had saved some money, but not enough to live in the style of my choosing for the rest of my life. I would have to work and, frankly, aside from being a model, I have no marketable skills. Don't judge me too harshly; I'm certainly not the first woman in history to marry in order to have a secure position in the world."

"But it didn't pan out?" Joanna asked.

"It was fine for the first year. Chandler was like a child with a new toy showing me off to everyone and enjoying the admiring glances of his male friends. But then the novelty began to fade. I was willing to do my share to be a supportive wife, but he really wasn't interested. Chandler is a bad combination of the possessive and the neglectful. He would become furious that I wanted to spend time with my own friends or travel anywhere without him, but he was hardly ever around. His business dominated his life, but he expected me to be instantly available whenever he took it into his head to come home."

"So you decided to get divorced and hired Ray Harris?" Joanna asked.

"I'm not sure I'd have had the courage to go through with the divorce except for Ray. Chandler would come around with his threats and bluster, but Ray would be here right next to me, calm and unflappable."

"According to Dianna Harris, you and Ray became lovers. Is that true?"

"Yes."

"How did Wright find out?"

"After the divorce, Chandler kept bothering me, and I got angry and told him how Ray was twice the man in bed that he was. That was foolish of me because he told Dianna the first chance he got, and that ended Ray's marriage. I don't think Ray ever forgave me for that. It was really what broke us up. He truly loved Dianna. His passion for me started to fade as soon as the divorce was settled. I guess I was no longer a woman in distress."

"Do you think that Chandler murdered Ray?" Joanna asked.

She gave a quick laugh. "I don't think Chandler could murder anyone. He's basically a coward. Oh, he's a big man with his real estate deals, and he browbeats his subordinates. But if things got physical, Chandler would skulk away."

"He could have hired someone to do it," Charles suggested.

"I suppose, but he'd still be afraid of being caught." She paused and looked across the room. "That also assumes that he'd care enough about losing me to take such a risk. I suspect that once he got over the shock of having someone leave him, he was actually pretty happy about it. Now he'd have the opportunity to move on to the next gullible girl."

"But you did cause him some financial pain," Joanna pointed out.

"No more than he can easily afford. For him, that was just the cost of doing business."

Joanna and Charles thanked Clarissa for her time.

"This is quite the log cabin," Charles commented when they reached the front door.

Clarissa Stevens laughed. "Isn't it? Chandler had the idea himself and paid through the nose to have it designed by some fancy architect. Just the type of overdone place that a boy from the city would think was appropriate to the country. That was the one thing I couldn't stand about Chandler. He never had any class."

"What do you think?" Charles asked Joanna as they drove south toward the center of Opalsville. "Still see Wright as a good suspect?"

She shrugged. "Just because his ex-wife thinks he was too gutless to be a killer doesn't mean she wasn't wrong about him. Even cowards sometimes get angry enough to kill. I think I want to judge the man for myself. I checked with the Opalsville Inn, and he's registered there for the next four days. I think I'll stop by tomorrow and have a chat with him."

"Want me to come along?"

"For protection?"

"No, I think you can handle that yourself. I figured you might want a second opinion from a man of age and experience."

"Feeling a bit of the arthritis, are we?"

"Actually, I've always wanted to meet a sleazy New York real estate developer in the flesh."

"I wouldn't want to deprive you of that opportunity."

Chapter Thirteen

After a quick early dinner, Joanna had to leave to attend a council meeting downtown because one of the items on the agenda was the police department's budget. Feeling at loose ends, Charles went into his study and looked over his work of the morning, but his mind soon drifted. The interviews of the afternoon had gotten him musing more than ever on the topic of betrayal. He wondered whether Harris's death had something to do with the betrayal of his marriage vows. Although Ray Harris had clearly had his own values that he staunchly supported, particularly getting a fair shake for women, he hadn't minded frequently taking his relationship with his female clients a step too far, at least in the eyes of their spouses. But according to their ex-wives, neither Carson nor Wright cared enough to resort to a violent attack on Harris. Of course, there could be an aggrieved husband out there that he and Joanna knew nothing about.

Charles mused on all this for several moments. He shook himself awake, realizing that he had dozed off. The long day and his workout at the gym were clearly catching up with him. He decided that he should take his garbage cans out to the curb before he was too tired to do so. The garbage truck came along so early in the morning that the cans had to be out the night before. Charles roused himself. He stood and stretched his muscles that had stiffened from his workout at the gym.

He walked through the kitchen and out the back door to where the garbage cans were located next to the porch. He lifted the one that was full. It was a metal can that he had brought with him from his old house, and a week's worth of garbage made it quite heavy. As he slowly made his way around the house and down the driveway to the curb, he once again, as he did most weeks, promised himself that he would soon replace the metal cans with plastic ones that had wheels.

When he had finally settled the heavy can down on the green space along the curb, Charles paused for an instant to look up and down the street. As he turned to head back up the driveway, a figure lurched out of the darkness and ran toward him. In the glow from the streetlight, he could see that the figure was dressed all in black and wearing a ski mask. When it got closer, the figure raised its right arm over its head. Without a moment to think, Charles pulled the lid off the garbage can and held it up in front of him. There was a loud clang as something metal hit the lid, sending a painful reverberation up his arm. Charles took a step backward as a second blow fell on the lid. There was a brief pause, as if his assailant was trying to work out a better strategy.

The next blow came from the side and almost tore the lid from Charles's grasp. But this time, he pivoted and rushed forward before the man could raise his weapon again. Charles charged right into him and had the satisfaction of hearing him grunt in surprise as he tumbled backward onto the ground. Charles risked lowering his shield for a moment and saw his opponent struggle to his feet and, once again, turn to confront him.

The figure in black came forward, but this time more cautiously. The blows were less powerful but more frequent. Charles found himself backing up and hoped that he wouldn't trip and fall onto his back. He suspected that could prove fatal. The lid itself was starting to buckle in the middle and would soon become almost useless as a shield. Charles was seriously considering throwing the bent lid at his opponent and making a run for it. After all, the very name of the Flight or Fight Gym pointed out that there were always two alternatives, and he liked his chances of being able to escape on foot.

He was just about to make his move when a voice from the porch of the house next door shouted, "What the hell is going on out there?"

Sam Baxter, his cranky next-door neighbor, had noticed the disturbance.

"Cut it out, whoever you are, or I'm going to call the police."

Charles heard the pounding of feet on the sidewalk, and when he slowly lowered the lid, his assailant had disappeared. Charles took a deep breath and leaned forward to rest his elbows on his knees. Now that the threat was over, a sudden surge of weariness had come over him.

"Oh, so it's you. I might have known."

Charles straightened and turned. Baxter stood behind him wearing a T-shirt that barely spanned his beer belly and a pair of shorts that went well below his knees.

"What are you trying to do? Wake up the whole neighborhood?"

"It was the size of a small bear," Charles replied.

Baxter looked around nervously. "What was?"

"The raccoon who tried to get in my garbage can. I had to fight him off with this," Charles said, holding up the battered lid.

"Okay, well I've got to get back inside," Baxter said, staring into the darkness nervously and heading back toward his house. "You should call animal control."

"I'll do that." Charles said. He decided that the can could do without its lid, which was so battered that it wouldn't fit anyway. He held it up in a ready position just in case he was attacked again on his way up the driveway.

Charles breathed a sigh of relief as he went into the kitchen and carefully locked the door behind him. Without pausing to think, he headed into his study and poured himself a large scotch. But when he tried to pick the glass up with his right hand, it shook uncontrollably and he had to use his left hand to get the liquid to his mouth. As he settled into his leather chair, he realized that his right arm was throbbing from having absorbed all of the blows of his attacker. It would no doubt be incredibly stiff in the morning.

Charles settled into the chair and tried to think objectively about what had happened. This had been no mugging because there had been no attempt made to get him to surrender his wallet. This had been an attack with the intent to do injury. And if the sound of the object banging on the can lid was an indication, the person had been using a pipe or something else made of metal. Charles thought about calling Joanna, but she was in the middle of what was probably a contentious council meeting and shouldn't be disturbed. He considered calling the police station to report the incident, but he wasn't sure whether it was a good idea to have news of the attack bruited all over town. In the end, he poured himself a second drink and fell into an exhausted slumber that only ended when Joanna appeared in the doorway.

"I suppose I should be flattered that when I'm not here at night you have to relieve your loneliness with alcohol," she said with a smile.

"I'm taking it purely for medicinal reasons," Charles mumbled, only half awake.

"That's what they all say."

"This time it's the truth," Charles said, and he told her the events of the evening.

As he went on, a concerned expression came over Joanna's face, and she sank down in the leather chair opposite him.

"You have no idea who attacked you?"

Charles shook his head. "None at all. It was most likely a man, but it could have been a big woman. It was too dark to tell. He or she was masked the whole time."

"Baxter saw it all?"

"No, he just heard the ruckus. I told him it was a gargantuan raccoon, and he seemed to believe me."

"And you didn't call the police?"

"I wasn't sure how to play it. My attacker was long gone, and there wasn't much evidence I could give to identify him or her."

"Okay, we'll leave it at that for now." Joanna paused. "You haven't ticked off anyone lately at the soup kitchen, the gym, or school."

"Although you apparently believe otherwise, I do not make deadly enemies wherever I go," Charles said with a hurt expression.

"Then it must have something to do with our investigation into Harris's murder. The good news is that it indicates we may be on the right track."

"That bad news is that I was almost killed."

Joanna nodded. "Yes. There is that."

Charles began to massage his arm.

"Does your arm hurt?" Joanna asked.

"I think I strained it holding off my attacker."

"I'll get you a couple of analgesics to go along with that scotch. You're going to need a good night's sleep. I want you ready to go tomorrow when we interrogate Chandler Wright."

"I'm game, as long as I can bring along my garbage can lid for protection."

Joanna gave him a hug. "Of course you can. You're my knight in shining armor. Even if it is a little dented right now."

Chapter Fourteen

Charles woke up early the next morning with a pain resembling a toothache in his right arm. It had disturbed him frequently during the night and kept him from sleeping soundly. After a hot shower and some more analgesics, he felt a bit better. When Joanna asked him how he was over breakfast, he downplayed the pain because he knew that she'd immediately make an appointment with an orthopedist if she suspected something was seriously wrong. Joanna was stoical about her own discomfort, but much more solicitous about any physical problems he might have. He hoped it was due to her generally caring nature and not because of their difference in age.

As she left for work, Joanna promised to call him once she'd set up a meeting with Chandler Wright, and Charles went into his study. The throb in his arm was distracting enough that he put his writing aside for the moment and sank into his leather chair. He had intended to pick up the novel he had been reading but found his mind wandering back to last night. Now that the excitement had somewhat worn off, he thought he'd be better able to consider the events of last night objectively.

He still felt that the attack indicated that the investigation he and Joanna had been conducting had gotten someone worried, but whom? Could they have dismissed Lester Baniff too quickly? After all, he was a computer expert, and maybe he had been able to make it appear that he was working in his office when he was actually busy stabbing Harris. Charles thought he was a bit short to be last night's attacker, but in the darkness and under stress, he wasn't sure that he'd been able to accurately gauge the figure's height. And there was always Stanley Carson, who was also rather short, but who might have been filled with rage at the loss and seduction of his wife. Even if Samantha Carson didn't think he cared enough about her to attack Harris, she could be wrong. Wives weren't always the most objective judges of their husbands' emotions. Finally, they may have rattled Chandler Wright's cage. Perhaps Clarissa Stevens had informed him that there was an investigation underway. He might have attacked Charles himself or gotten a hired thug to do it in order to derail the investigation. Finally, it was always remotely possible that Clarissa Stevens herself had been the attacker. She was certainly tall enough, although Charles couldn't think of a reason why she would have been disturbed by their questions.

Charles began to consider all the possibilities until he drifted off into a light doze. When the phone rang, he was so startled that it took him a moment to realize where he was, and he had to scramble for the phone.

"Hope I didn't wake you," Joanna said.

"No. I was just lost in thought."

"Hmm. Well, I've got an appointment set up with Chandler Wright at the Opalsville Inn in an hour. "Do you still feel up to attending?"

"Of course," Charles said, trying to sound upbeat even though the ache in his arm had returned. "I'll meet you at the station."

"I can swing by and pick you up at home if you'd prefer."

"No. I may go on to the college this afternoon, so I might as well have my car at the station."

"Okay. See you in twenty minutes."

Charles rushed out into the kitchen and made himself a peanut butter and jelly sandwich to take with him. If he did go on to the college, he'd eat it at his desk. This was pure comfort food, and the way he was feeling at the moment, comfort was going to be the name of the game for today.

He arrived at the police station right on time, and Joanna came out immediately and took him through to the police parking lot.

"How did Wright sound when you spoke with him?" Charles asked as they settled into her car.

"Extremely polite. He sounded like a man who was trying to pretend that there wasn't a dishonest bone in his body."

"Next he'll be telling you that he's a legitimate businessman."

"The problem is that even the legitimate businesses sometimes skirt the law."

Charles smiled. "Having one of your cynical mornings."

"White-collar crime is under investigated and minimally prosecuted, and yet, overall, it probably does more social damage than muggers on the street."

"Well, if Wright did kill Harris, this is certainly more than a white-collar crime, and he may have done something to give himself away."

Joanna nodded. "Let's hope so."

When they arrived at the parking lot of the Opalsville Inn, Charles was once again reminded of the woman he had watched die in that lot a couple of years ago. Although she had been seriously strange in her view of life, he still harbored some fond thoughts of her, and never came to the inn without experiencing a sense of loss.

Joanne and Charles went into the lobby and walked up to the reception desk where they asked a young woman wearing a badge that said her name was Linda if she would contact the room of Chandler Wright and let him know that the police were waiting downstairs to question him. The woman made a call and said that Mr. Wright would be down shortly. Joanna asked if they could use the room off the lobby for a brief conference, and Linda said she didn't see any problem with that.

Charles wasn't sure exactly what he had expected Chandler Wright to look like, but he had probably leaned toward a husky, torpedo-shaped character exuding physical menace. But the man who came down that stairs was tall and rangy, more a shortstop than a football player. He had a full head of brown hair flecked with gray and was dressed in a knit shirt and chinos. He looked like any reasonably fit executive on his way out to play a round of golf.

Charles and Joanna introduced themselves. Wright shook hands and gave each of them a cordial smile.

"When I heard that Harris had been killed, I knew it would be only a matter of time before you got around to speaking with me."

"Why is that?" Joanna asked.

"Because I was never shy about expressing how I felt about him."

"Why don't we go to the room off the lobby for our chat." Joanna said. With Joanna in the lead, the three of them headed into what was called the card room in the rear of the lobby.

Wright settled down on one side of a card table across from Joanna, while Charles sat off to the side.

"You must have been rather unhappy with the vigorous way that Ray Harris represented your wife during the divorce?" Joanna asked.

Wright shrugged. "I suppose it was to be expected. He was good at what he did, and that was his job. I certainly wished that things had turned out a bit more equitably."

"You seem very philosophical about it all right now, but isn't it true that you threatened Harris at the time of the divorce?"

"If you listen carefully to what people say, you'll know that I never threatened physical harm of any kind. However, I did threaten to damage his law firm."

"By getting local companies to take their legal business elsewhere?"

"I'm not without influence in this part of the world, and as far as I know, using that influence isn't illegal."

Joanna nodded. "Was the outcome of your divorce the only reason you were furious with Ray Harris?"

"What do you mean?"

"Isn't it also true that he slept with Clarissa while the divorce was going on?"

Charles thought that Wright must have made an effort to control his expression, only the slight compression of his lips indicated a flash of emotion. He managed to turn it into a wry smile.

"Not very professional of him, was it? I thought about trying to get him disbarred but decided that it would be better to destroy his business than have him get a slap on the wrist for unethical conduct."

"Maybe you got impatient with the effort to destroy his business and decided to take care of it in a quicker and more direct way?"

He shook his head slowly and gave her a complacent smile. "I'm a very patient man. That's how I got to where I am today."

"Where were you last Monday night at around eight?"

"At a meeting of the friends of the Opalsville Library. They had a small reception for the more generous donors. I was there from seven until almost nine. I'm sure any number of local notables saw me there, including the mayor."

Joanna nodded and jotted down a note on the file in front of her.

"I'll check into that."

"Please do."

"Thank you for your cooperation, Mr. Wright. We'll be in touch if we have any further questions."

Wright stood up and looked down on the two of them.

"As you can imagine, I have no regrets that the man is dead. But I had nothing to do with his murder, and as I'm sure you have discovered, any number of men had reasons similar to mine for killing him."

"Of course, he's right," Joanna said, after Wright had walked away.

"But we've followed up on all the ones we know about, and none of them have panned out."

"I'm going to ask Sharon Thorpe to dig further into Harris's past cases and see if she can find anything that might bring a new suspect to the surface. We don't know how many women he was involved with who might have ex-husbands still harboring a grievance."

"I suppose," Charles said.

Joanna gave him a sharp glance. "You don't think this is the right way to go?"

"I can't think of a better one. But I just have a feeling that we've got something turned around here."

"If inspiration strikes, let me know."

"You'll be the first."

Chapter Fifteen

W hen Joanna dropped him off back at the station, Charles got in his car and drove up to the college. The ache in his arm seemed to have subsided or else he was becoming accustomed to the pain. In any event, he thought that being active would distract him from the discomfort, rather than sitting at home brooding on his condition. He had parked his car and was about to go up the stairs of the English Department building when someone called his name. He turned and saw Jonathan Royce walking across the campus toward him.

"Good morning, Charles," Royce said, shaking his hand. "I thought you were retired."

"I retain an office here and come in when the mood strikes me."

Royce glanced across the campus. "It certainly is a beautiful spot. Makes you think that being in college is an idyllic experience. Although, when I recall my own college days, there was plenty of stress and anxiety."

"Every age has its own trials and tribulations. When we're old, we tend to forget about the pain of youth, and when we're young, we don't know the troubles to come."

Royce laughed. "Sounds like you're having a challenging day. Is the Harris investigation getting you down?"

"It is proving challenging."

"My wife, Mona, tells me that you spoke to Dianna Harris."

"That's right."

"Since Mona tells her everything, you're probably aware then that my wife and I have been going through a difficult patch."

"She mentioned that your wife approached her about having Ray represent her in a divorce."

He nodded. "We've since decided to get marriage counseling and try to work things out."

"According to Dianna, your wife wanted Ray to represent her, and he refused."

"That's right. Even though technically it would be perfectly ethical, Ray didn't feel comfortable being in an adversarial relationship with me." Royce smiled. "Ray could be a cutthroat lawyer, but he did draw the line at jeopardizing a friendship. He gave Dianna the names of a couple of other lawyers to pass on to Mona, which was fine. But as I said, we've decided to try to reconcile. Work has been really challenging for the last year or so, and it's taken up much of my time. Mona, quite rightly, felt neglected, and I'm trying to rectify that now."

"I'm sure work is the reason you're on the campus today."

He rolled his eyes. "I've taken a position on President Dawson's advisory council. It takes up a lot of time, but Opal College is an important client."

"College committees can be pure drudgery. I don't envy you."

"You have to take the work where you can get it."

"Well, I hope things work out between you and your wife."

"Recognizing that there's a problem is the important first step, and I think with some professional help, we'll work it through."

Charles walked up the stairs to the building thinking about how many threatened and failed marriages he'd heard about in the last few days. His own first marriage had, in retrospect, not been a resounding success, and he reminded himself once again to make every effort to do better with Joanna.

As he walked into the English Department office to pick up his mail, Yuri came down the hall to his office and greeted him.

"I have good news," Yuri announced. "I have managed to get two highly competent adjuncts to teach your courses for next year, so we won't be needing to disturb your retirement."

"That is good news."

"We are setting up a hiring committee to find a permanent replacement for you. As you know, this has not been an overwhelming success in the past. Your first replacement was murdered, and the next two ended up incarcerated, partly due to your own involvement in the investigation."

"I'm aware of that," Charles said dryly.

"Because of that, President Dawson has requested that you serve on the hiring committee. That way, if there are any issues, we can head them off at the intersection."

Charles frowned. It took him a second to capture the meaning. "You mean head them off at the pass."

Now it was Yuri's turn to look puzzled. "Where does that phrase come from?"

"Watch some old westerns and you'll figure it out."

"I doubt very much that I will ever do that."

"Why does Dawson think that my presence on the committee will be helpful? He surely doesn't want me to do background checks on each candidate."

"I guess he feels you have good intuitions when it comes to spotting future criminals."

"He can't require me to do it, you know. I am retired."

"Ah, yes. Well, we have been experiencing a bit of a space shortage lately, and it is possible that you might be asked to move into a smaller office that you will have to share with three or four adjuncts."

"That sounds like a threat."

Yuri shrugged. "I am simply reporting what I have been told. I'm sure that if you were helping the college hire new faculty, this problem would disappear."

"Yes, I'm sure it would." Charles paused and realized that he would miss having the same space he'd occupied for the last thirty years. A big chunk of his professional and creative life had taken place within those four walls, and he was hesitant to let it go just yet. "Okay, tell the president that I will serve on the committee, but I don't like being extorted."

"Such an ugly word, Charles, for what is essentially a reciprocal arrangement. You know the old saying, you scratch my back and I'll wash yours."

Charles didn't bother to correct him.

"At any rate, we are having an organizational meeting of the hiring committee in the dean's conference room at three o'clock tomorrow afternoon. Will you be able to make it?"

Reluctantly, Charles nodded.

"Don't be so down, my friend, you might find this an enjoyable experience."

"Going through a hundred resumes is not my idea of enjoyment."

"But you will be making a contribution to the college that will last for decades to come."

"I'll try to think of it that way," Charles said as he turned and headed for his office.

He sat behind his desk fuming for several minutes. There was hardly any physical violence in academic life, but there were many opportunities to feel that you had been battered. After a few minutes, however, he began to think that having some say in his replacement might be a good thing. He'd have an opportunity to direct the department's American literature offerings in a way that might be more consistent with his own approach. Perhaps he'd be fortunate enough to discover a young scholar with whom he had something in common. A friendship with someone younger would not be an altogether bad thing. Too often as you got older, your circle of friends began to become limited to your own age group, and they simply reinforced your antiquated view of the world. Getting more in touch with the latest scholarship in his field would be a good thing, even if he were no longer a productive scholar.

Putting the whole matter to one side, he began to eat his sandwich and think instead about the Harris murder. Although he thought Joanna was showing due diligence in having Sharon Thornby dig deeper into Harris's history of divorce cases, he doubted that an angry husband from five or ten years ago was likely to have suddenly decided to even the score with Ray. Murdering someone in almost broad daylight smacked of desperation, not of a plan developed meticulously over the years. Maybe Dianna Harris had something to gain from her ex-husband's death. Since they didn't have any children, he might not be the first guy to leave his former wife as his heir. Although Dianna had seemed to still have considerable affection for Ray, it would also have been easy for her to get close enough to stab him without his expecting it. That would be something for Joanna to look into further.

Thinking about Joanna reminded him that he had to prepare dinner and so he should go home to see what was available for tonight's meal. Harboring mixed feelings about his visit to the college, he locked up his desk and the door to his office and headed home.

Chapter Sixteen

Charles and Joanna were sitting in the inglenook by the kitchen fireplace savoring a small scotch each. Charles had a chicken salad prepared for dinner, which seemed appropriate on what had been a rather warm August day. Fortunately, the central air conditioning installed by the previous owner worked well, so the house remained comfortable in all seasons of the year. Some old New Englanders still swore that air conditioning wasn't necessary this far north, but Charles considered this more a testimony to their rugged character than to their awareness of the temperature and humidity.

"Did you get a chance to speak with Sharon Thornby about digging into Harris's old cases?" Charles asked.

Joanna nodded and stretched out on the bench, as if trying to relieve stress in her back. "She'll do it when she gets around to it. Right now, she's more focused on doing a job search."

"She's been fired?" Charles asked in surprise.

"Not exactly. But it appears that Jonathan Royce has decided that the firm should no longer handle divorce work, and since that's what Thornby is interested in doing, she's planning to move on."

"He's not going to replace Harris with a new partner?"

"That's what he told her."

"Why the sudden change of direction?"

"Well, I got the impression that Harris was the driving force behind doing divorce work. According to Thornby, Royce has always felt that it was too confrontational for a staid firm like Barlow, Harris, and Royce. Now that he's the only senior partner, he plans to take the firm in the direction of doing more estate planning, wills, contracts, and business law."

"I had a chat with Royce today up on campus, and he didn't mention it to me. Of course, our conversation was more focused on his attempts to save his marriage."

Charles went on to give Joanna a summary of their conversation.

"So it sounds like Royce really appreciated the fact that Ray had refused to represent his wife," Joanna said.

"Yeah. I guess that Mona's threat of divorce got him to pay attention to his relationship with his wife in a new way. I think Jonathan Royce felt something of a debt of gratitude for the way Harris handled the situation. But I can see why he might not want to take on another divorce lawyer. After all, Harris was quite a flamboyant character and did attract enemies."

Joanna gazed across the room. "If Sharon Thornby doesn't come up with something helpful from Harris's past, I'm not sure where to go next with this case."

"I was wondering, who was Ray Harris's heir. That might give us some idea of who had a motive to kill him."

"I'll look into it. Did you have someone special in mind?"

"Dianna Harris. She was probably going to inherit when they were married. Maybe he never changed his will. That would give her a good motive."

"I suppose. I'm not sure I see her as a killer, but right now I'd just be happy to find someone with a motive and no alibi. Did you learn anything else at the college?"

Charles frowned. "That I'm going to be serving on the search committee to select my replacement."

"How did that happen?"

Charles described his conversation with Yuri.

Joanna grinned. "Yuri might not have much of a grasp of the vernacular, but he's a pretty clever guy. I'll bet he suggested to President Dawson that you be added to that committee."

"Why? To punish me because my past replacements turned into a murderers row?"

"Partly, perhaps. But also because he has confidence that you can spot a rotten apple when you see one. No offense, but in my experience, most academics are like babes in the woods when it comes to seeing what people are really like. They may be able to critique a résumé and evaluate someone's teaching, but great judges of character they are not."

"So I should be flattered?"

"A little bit. Also, it will give you a chance to help determine who replaces you. Doesn't that mean anything to you?"

"I was thinking about that earlier. At least it will give me something of a chance to see that American literature continues in a similar direction to the way it has under me."

"Right. It's your chance to leave a mark on the institution that will long outlive you. A sort of legacy."

"A legacy? That makes me feel old."

"Don't you want to be remembered?"

"Yeah, as the guy who lived to be a hundred and ten."

Joanna laughed and stood up. "Well then, we'd better have dinner. You need to keep your strength up."

Chapter Seventeen

After breakfast the next morning, Charles went into his study and returned to working on his book. The pain in his arm was much diminished, and he found that he had a lot of pent-up ideas that he wanted to get down on the page. His story was focusing more and more on betrayal as it related to friendship. Although the plot was rather different, he suspected that he was inspired by one of his favorite Raymond Chandler novels, *The Long Goodbye*. After love between a man and a woman, the bond of friendship between men was perhaps the deepest human relationship, and Charles thought his novel should try to examine that through the lens of a murder mystery. He was finding more and more as he wrote that the mystery genre could be used as a legitimate means of telling a story that would be just as important as any novel by a so-called serious novelist. He was under no illusion that critics or scholars would see it that way, but he cared little about that. The only people he was interested in impressing were his readers.

He wrote steadily until he stopped for an early lunch. After lunch, he headed out for the gym. His organizational meeting of the search committee was scheduled for today at three, and he wanted to be physically tired or else he would be twitchy the whole time. The ability of academics to talk every subject to death twice over was something he could only tolerate if his brain was filled with post exercise endorphins.

Charles pushed himself particularly hard on the treadmill, running longer and faster than usual. He knew he'd pay for it with stiffness the next morning when he got out of bed, but the exercise high would help him get through the afternoon. He made a quick stop at home to shower and change clothes. Then he headed out to the campus. He was walking down the hall to the dean's office when someone touched him on his shoulder. He turned and was confronted by the rotund figure of Travis Merriman, the arms manufacturer he had met at the reception the other night.

"Ah, Professor Bentley, we meet again," the man said with a phlegmy chortle.

"Apparently so."

"You don't seem happy to see me."

"I'm just in a rush on my way to a meeting."

"So am I. I'm on the president's special committee for fundraising. We've been meeting the entire week. That's the only reason I haven't returned to Texas."

"I'm not surprised that a large donor like yourself is asked for input on fundraising."

"Yes. Money does buy influence, among other things."

"Thanks for suggesting to President Dawson that I be more involved in fundraising."

Merriman smiled. "I could see how much you enjoyed yourself at that reception. The least I could do for a man who threatened me with a knife is to see that he had many other such pleasant evenings."

"There was no threat. We were just having a conversation."

"Have it your own way. But there's no point in having power unless you can use it. Don't you agree?"

Before Charles could answer, Jonathan Royce walked past. He looked surprised to see Charles and Merriman together. They both greeted the lawyer as he passed.

Merriman watched him go by. "Royce is on the president's committee as well because he's the college counsel."

Charles nodded. "So aside from influence, what do you get out of giving a big donation?"

The man shrugged his heavy shoulders. "It's different for every donor. For me it's simple vanity, seeing my name over a door dedicating an auditorium to me."

"Your legacy," Charles said, recalling his earlier conversation with Joanna.

"If you like. No one is remembered for very long, but words on a wall mean you'll be remembered longer than most. There is a certain satisfaction in that. But for some, having influence is really the only thing. Do you know Chandler Wright?"

Charles nodded.

"Rumor has it that he's been pushing for the last few months to have Jonathan Royce replaced as the college attorney. I heard it was actually going to happen, but then a couple of weeks ago, Wright suddenly stopped his lobbying." Merriman sighed. "There's a man who doesn't care how he's remembered."

"Some people don't. Having power is everything."

Merriman nodded and put out a pudgy hand. "If you're ever down in Texas Charles, look me up. Maybe we can find out what really happens when you bring a knife to a gunfight."

Charles reluctantly shook the damp hand and hurried down the hall to his meeting.

* * * *

TWO HOURS LATER, CHARLES finally staggered out of the hiring committee meeting. It had truly been as harrowing as he had expected. The vice president of academic affairs had rattled on for almost half an hour about the importance of the endeavor they were about to embark on, as if they were selecting the next United States president rather than an assistant professor of English. Yuri had bumbled through a malapropism laden discourse on what the qualifications for the position had to be and went into great detail on the high security measures necessary for protecting the privacy of all candidates. After all of this came the grueling labor of actually formulating the ad for the job position. Letting four English professors loose on a writing assignment was like setting out a rabbit in front of a course of greyhounds. Charles let his colleagues argue themselves into exhaustion before finally stepping in and settling all of the little disputes.

As Charles walked across the campus in the dimming light of the late afternoon, he found his mind going back not to the committee discussion he had just witnessed, but to his conversation with Travis Merriman. He knew something significant had been said at the time, but he hadn't had time to fully digest it. Although his mind was tired, he slowly began absorbing the significant point Merriman had made. Royce was in real danger of losing perhaps his firm's most significant client because of the dispute between Harris and Wright. The only thing that had ended Wright's persecution of the law firm had been Harris's death.

"Wait up, Charles!"

Charles turned and saw Jonathan Royce coming along at a rapid pace. He stopped a few feet away.

"I guess we've both had pretty hectic meetings today," Royce said with a smile.

"Mine was mind numbing. I'm sure I've lost brain cells that can never be revived."

The man laughed. "Lawyers are immune to that. We put up with it every day."

"I suppose that's true. Professors are usually the ones doing the boring, rather than the ones being bored."

Royce nodded and turned serious. "I saw you speaking with Travis Merriman earlier. I was surprised that you knew him."

"We met at a fundraiser recently."

"The man is quite the gossip," Royce said, and studied Charles's face.

"A lot of rich people are in my experience."

"Yes. Well, I spoke to him before the meeting began, and he told me that he mentioned the problem I'd been having with Chandler Wright."

"You mean his attempt to have your firm replaced as school counsel?"

"Yes. I'm sure you realize that would have had very serious consequences for Barlow, Harris, and Royce."

"I imagine it would. But I guess that problem has been obviated by Harris's death. Hasn't it?"

"But I also realize this also makes me a suspect in Ray's death."

"It certainly gives you a clear motive. I'm sure the firm is everything to you, and you'd do anything to protect it."

Royce glanced away, and Charles thought he could see tears well up in his eyes.

"I tried to explain that to Ray. That he should resign for the sake of the firm. He could always set up his own practice."

"But he wouldn't do it?"

Royce shook his head. "He said he wasn't going to give in to intimidation by some cheap thug."

"Couldn't you have gone your own way without Harris?" Charles asked.

"You mean put out my own shingle. Of course, but then it wouldn't be Barlow, Harris, and Royce. And why should I leave the firm when it was Ray's fault that we were in this predicament.

Wright would never have been so furious if Ray hadn't slept with his wife. He never did have any self-control."

"But he was your friend, and he refused to represent your wife in divorce proceedings."

"I know he was my friend."

"But you had to kill him."

Royce's eyes fixed on Charles and turned cold. His right hand went behind his back and appeared gripping what looked to be a hunting knife. Charles felt his spine quiver and barely suppressed a strong desire to run. He realized that there was actually no one around to see this event play out.

"Don't be silly, Jonathan. I've already called Joanna and told her about my conversation with Merriman. Killing me will serve no purpose."

"I don't think you have, Charles. You wouldn't have called during the meeting, and I've been following you since you left the dean's office. You haven't made any calls."

Charles desperately tried to come up with another angle.

"All Merriman's story does is give you a motive. There's still no evidence that you murdered Harris. No one saw you, so we have no proof."

"But once I'm the prime suspect, you'll dig and dig, and you might find something. Even if you don't, word will get around that I was a suspect in Ray's death. That alone will be enough to destroy the firm. I can't let you tell anyone what you know."

Charles tried to sound calm and reasonable. "It will come out anyway, Jonathan."

"Maybe not. That's a chance I'll just have to take."

Royce took a long step forward and his right hand, which was holding the knife, thrust forward toward Charles's chest. Charles reached out with his left hand and just managed to grab Royce's wrist. He held on desperately, while his right hand swiftly removed the knife from his pants pocket and his thumb clicked the short blade into place. As Royce struggled to free his hand, Charles plunged his knife into Royce's forearm until he felt the blade hit bone. Jonathan Royce gave a cry of surprise and pain. He dropped the knife, which Charles kicked away. Royce fell to one knee, covering the wound in his arm with his left hand.

Charles stood over him a moment, waiting to see if he was going to attack again. Then he took out his phone and called Joanna.

• • • •

TWO DAYS LATER, JOANNA and Charles were sitting in front of the kitchen fireplace sipping scotch.

"So did Jonathan Royce confess to murdering Ray Harris?" Charles asked.

"He did. The knife he tried to kill you with turned out to be the same one he used on Ray. Forensics found evidence of Ray's blood. When we confronted him with that, he broke down and admitted everything. You know, you were right, if he hadn't attacked you, we'd have had a very hard time making a case against him."

"But in a way, Royce was right to. Even if he only came under suspicion, the rumor mill would have tarnished his reputation and seriously damaged Barlow, Harris, and Royce."

"Still, losing the firm would have been better than going to jail."

Charles shook his head. "Not for Jonathan Royce. For him the work was everything. The firm was more important than his freedom, his marriage, and ultimately friendship."

Joanna reached over and touched Charles's face. "You came pretty close to being killed."

"Not really. As long as you bring a knife to a knife fight, you've got an even chance. But there's a guy out in Texas that I don't plan to visit any time soon."

"You've had a pretty eventful birthday week."

"Especially with the hiring committee and all that."

Joanna grinned. "That wasn't what I meant."

"I know, but that may be the most important thing I did all week. Because that could turn out to be my legacy, my footsteps in the sand."

"Your legacy will also be here with me and with Amy. Don't forget that."

Charles leaned over and gave her a kiss. "I won't," he said softly.

Thank you for reading *A Killer Birthday.* If you enjoyed this book, you might also like the first six novels in the Charles Bentley series: *A Body in My Office, Death of a Survivalist, To Die for Art, Death by Karma, The Final Lecture,* and *A Deadly Path to Enlightenment.*

To see descriptions of all my books and easily purchase them, please go to www.glenebisch.com and click on the "books" pages at the top. You may offer opinions on my "contact" page at the same website. If you would like to receive my newsletter, please send me your email address, and I'll add your name to my mailing list.

As always, if you enjoyed the book, a review on Amazon is appreciated.

Made in the USA
Columbia, SC
09 November 2023

25817556R00048